The Alphabet Wars

The Alphabet Wars

Raf Erzeel

DIADEM BOOKS

Published by Diadem Books

For information, please contact:

Diadem Books
Ocean Surf
CLASHNESSIE
IV27 4JF
Scotland UK

www.diadembooks.com

This book is a work of fiction. Names, characters and places are products of the author's imagination. Any resemblance is entirely coincidental.

ISBN: 978-0-9559852-0-1

Contents

Part I

The Alphabet Wars

The Alphabet Wars

Dublyu, General of the Roman army, was staring blankly into the flames of the dwindling campfire, worrying about the impending battle. The murmur of the soldiers' voices around him had blended with the crackling of the logs, the soft encouragements of the wind in the trees and the absentminded tapping of his own stick against the rock he was sitting on. Dublyu's mind was not exclusively on military things, though; his daughter Bee was a big worry, too, what with the poor state of health he had had to leave her in when he set out on this campaign, supposedly the decisive stage in the Alphabet Wars that had been going on for over thirty years now.

In truth, the conflict had a much longer history – and probably an even longer future. What was generally known as the Alphabet Wars was a relatively local conflict between the Roman, Greek, Phoenician, Hebrew and Etruscan scripts. Over the years, almost any permutation of coalitions had come and gone – they never lasted long, as anyone with any sense knew that the battle was one for a monopoly. No alphabet was prepared to share the prize – a position of dominance throughout Europe and the shores of the Mediterranean – with any of the others. It simply wasn't workable to combine two alphabets, so it was a situation of everyone for themselves. The longest coalition had been the one between the Roman and Greek alphabets, and together they had decisively defeated (or rather annihilated) the Phoenician and Etruscan alphabets. The irony was that in doing so, they had obliterated their immediate forefathers – the original Greek alphabet had been modelled on the Phoenician one, and the Etruscan (itself based on the Greek) gave rise to the Roman. And now the two biggest players were taking on each other. They had both decided to ignore Hebrew for the time being – it was becoming less and less ambitious anyway, and seemed happy with its own little niche.

Luckily, mused Dublyu, there was hardly any doubt anymore as to the dominance of the Roman alphabet in Europe and all along the shores of the Mediterranean. It was only one step away from the monopoly it had long dreamed of – if only Greek could be defeated.

While he conjured up the face of Tau, his counterpart at the head of the Greek army, and wondered about the reputation as a ruthless brute that Tau had acquired, it was Bee's lovely features that kept superimposing themselves on the image Dublyu was trying to focus on. He fervently hoped that the mysterious illness that had so weakened her over the past few weeks was finally showing signs of releasing its powerful grip. He couldn't bear the thought that his daughter, his own ink and strokes, might succumb to the illness and be lost forever. His wife Vee would fall apart, that much he was certain of, and he could only guess at the reaction of his son Aey.

Dublyu cursed himself for allowing his mind to wander to his family; that was a luxury for an army commander, and he shouldn't be indulging in it. His mind should be firmly and exclusively on the upcoming battle and on his adversary.

Tau was hardly a stranger to him: during the time of the Roman-Greek coalition the two of them had been in close contact, and – even though it would not be wise to say so now – they had been fairly good friends, enjoying each other's company outside the professional field. He had even got to know Tau's family. So Dublyu could be pretty certain that at this precise moment, also, Tau's mind would be wandering to his loved ones, and not be obsessively focused on the fight in hand. It had to be said, though, that he feared Tau's ruthless side: in strategy and in battle, Tau was well-known for his unshakable concentration and steely nerve. Privately, Dublyu had always known that Tau was the better general; publicly, he would never admit to that, and he would always stress the advantage he held over Tau in knowing the general's mind.

♣

The crackling campfire of a few hours ago was not much more than glowing embers now, and Dublyu poked them with his stick. Sparks flew up, hundreds of little fireflies against the dark that surrounded him. He realised that the entire camp had fallen silent, that he was the only one still about. It soothed his nerves. Somehow, the silence and the loneliness were a comfort to him. Knowing that all around him, all his soldiers, all the brave letters, from the lowliest lower-case Aey to the highest capital Zed, were getting the crucial rest they needed on the eve of the most important battle of the entire war, bolstered his confidence. He was proud of his army, and he knew that whatever the outcome of tomorrow's fight, he would always be proud of them. He could see them now, lined up in battle formation, all the ranks of different fonts and sizes, ready to give the Greek letters the fight of their lives.

The sun glinted off the helmets of the seventh division, all of them crack troops, all Arial Aeys. They were impatiently awaiting Dublyu's order to attack. The plan was for them to rush straight towards the Greek army, then veer off to the right before engaging the enemy, and take their attention off the sixth division breaking away from the back of the Roman army to perform a drawn-out movement to the left. If the Greeks could be distracted just long enough for the sixth to get to the cover of the woods, they could then go all the way to the right flank of the Greek army and surprise them there when the main battle was under way. Dublyu raised his right arm, and brought it down in an elegant sweeping movement: the signal for the seventh to start their feigned attack. They set off as one letter; their coordinated swift move was like poetry – a brash limerick, completely unexpected. He could see the Greek command waver momentarily before orders were given to hold positions and parry the enemy attack. But then the seventh division swept to the right, at a right angle with the combined Greek army. Dublyu could sense the consternation in both the Greek troops and their leaders. He looked around to the sixth division, and saw to his satisfaction that they were on the move – exactly on cue. It was working – the Greeks didn't notice the covert manoeuvre; their full attention was on the maverick actions of the seventh division.

Dublyu jerked back awake – he had dropped off, and his dream proved that he was more focused on the battle than he had suspected. The surprise move that he had dreamt about was as much a surprise to him as to the Greeks, though. He had been worried sick because the only strategy that he'd been able to come up with was a straightforward massed attack. The idea might just work... He drew a few sketchy lines in the dust around what was now barely the ghost of a campfire. If he could position his army near to the woods there, the sixth would indeed be able to disappear into the woods in a minimum of time. This was it – the extra element that might just force a victory. The only thing he needed to do was to wake up the leaders of the sixth and seventh divisions and brief them on the plan.

♣

There was confident calm in the Greek camp after the last whispered discussions about Tau's earlier speech had died down. The general had the uncanny knack of making his speeches rousing and reassuring at the same time. All the letters in the Greek army agreed on one thing at least: Tau had succeeded in inspiring them with his obvious confidence. Victory would be theirs tomorrow, that much was certain. Tau was both feared and revered by his officers and the enlisted letters – his reputation went before him, and all kinds of stories, the one more unbelievable than the other, were recounted again and again, and each time the claims about the general's qualities and idiosyncrasies became a little more outrageous. He was said to be scrupulously fair, but also ruthless and incredibly strict. Rumours abounded of him having erased letters of all ranks for showing even the slightest disrespect to him or to the cause. Cowardice would provoke terrible punishments for the soldier's family before the culprit was brutally killed by dismemberment.

Tau was acutely aware of his reputation, and actively encouraged the rumours that fed it. In truth, he had never subjected any of his troops to unreasonable punishments, and would never dream of targeting their families. His wife and children always said he was a big softie, and his strict demeanour as a general was indeed an act more than anything else. Yet Tau was convinced that a general needed to be seen as hard and unfeeling, but also fair, in order to be respected. Respect led to obedience, and obedience was the basic requirement for military success. Only if a general could be absolutely certain that his commands would be executed, could he be effective in planning a strategy and applying it on the battlefield.

Tau knew that his speech had been the best he had ever made, even though he was not half as confident as he had made believe. The letters had cheered, and the confidence he had instilled in them had flowed back to him, lifting him up. Now that all the excitement had died down, he was trying to persuade himself that he actually did have good reason to be confident. His opponent Dublyu had always been less competent a general, and certainly lacked the strategic brilliance required for greatness. In tomorrow's battle, the Roman army would undoubtedly rely on a simple massed attack – that had almost always been Dublyu's 'strategy'. The only variations that Tau had ever witnessed were two- and three-pronged attacks, and then only after stubborn insistence by his officers. No, good old reliable Dublyu would not surprise him. The only question in his mind was whether he should go in for some fancy strategy, or simply rely on his troops' courage and numerical advantage to stop the first wave of the Roman attack and then trust his instinct to come up with an inspired move to plunge the Romans into chaos. He was renowned for his brilliant strategies thought out on the spot, in the middle of the battle; and because he knew he could rely on his troops to do exactly as they were told, the strategies tended to be highly successful.

Tau could almost hear his lovely wife Zeta say 'Don't worry, Arktos dear, you'll come up with something, as you always do.'

She would always call him Arktos, bear, in private. Her soft-spoken kindness and her unwavering and unconditional trust in him made a combination that would almost move him to tears. If only he could be with her tonight – she would comfort him and hold him, and keep him from worrying. He closed his eyes and imagined how Zeta would have put the children to bed and would now be saying her prayers before turning in for the night herself. 'Sleep tight, dearest,' he said out loud, taking himself by surprise. It was a good thing there was no-one to overhear him; a few careless words like these could well destroy his reputation. The general shook his head to clear his mind – he shouldn't be thinking of his family now; such thoughts only distracted him from the job in hand. Yet he couldn't prevent the image of his two young daughters, Epsilon and Phi, from flashing into his head. Then he concentrated on the upcoming battle again. The unconditional confidence of his wife persuaded him that he would trust his competence once again, even if tomorrow's battle was to be the most important he had ever fought. He would decide on the strategy after the first Roman wave of attack.

♣

Historians would later neglect to describe the beauty of the morning of the battle, and have eyes only for the military aspects and for the eventual outcome. They would, of course, put the battle into perspective, analyse its importance in the whole of the Alphabet Wars, and inevitably romanticise the event, failing to mention the cruel loss of so many letters.

The truth of the matter was that at dawn that morning, the world seemed to be making an extra effort: the colour of the sky was stunning, the scattered wisps of mist coming off the ground accentuating the glow of the fresh sunlight. Gradually, as the sun rose, the hills turned from dark, threatening forms into friendly, wooded landmarks. Birdsong momentarily drowned out the cold, matter-of-fact sounds coming from the two army camps – though no doubt the soldiers were unaware of this. The only thing on their minds was the nervousness that preceded any battle; yet today especially, they all seemed to be aware of the crucial importance of their individual performance. Each and every letter knew what they were supposed to do, and intended to fulfil their duty.

The activity in both the Greek and Roman encampments was consistent with imminent battle, and the sound of trumpets, pipes and drums was much louder than the earlier peaceful birdsong. Yet two full hours after sunrise there were no actual battle formations, let alone any fighting. The soldiers were becoming impatient, and slightly worried. Something was going on, and they were taken aback by the unfamiliarity of it all.

As if by arrangement, a small group of letters on horseback emerged from each camp at exactly the same moment, carrying a banner signifying negotiation rather than attack. It was clear for anyone to see that at the centre of the two groups were generals Tau and Dublyu. The groups met exactly halfway between the encampments, and Tau and Dublyu dismounted and walked towards each other, both unarmed. Under the watchful eye of, by now, not only the small groups of bodyguards, but the entire armies, the generals greeted each other and started to talk.

They lowered their voices to a whisper, so that no-one could overhear their conversation.

'Dublyu, my friend,' Tau started, 'I would hate to have you think that I did not at least make an attempt at a negotiated peace.'

'You took the words right out of my mouth, dear Tau,' Dublyu replied. 'It suddenly came to me this morning how utterly senseless this war is. Why can't our two alphabets coexist peacefully? I mean, we are even related. It's the politicians that seem intent on continuing the conflict, but they are not here to fight, are they?'

'All too true, my friend.' Tau hesitated for a moment, and then slowly shook his head. 'But we both know that, in spite of what our soldiers may think, our individual power is all but negligible. The politicians want this war and this battle, and they shall have it.'

Dublyu just lowered his head and didn't say anything. He just felt very sad all of a sudden. In spite of all his enthusiasm last night about his strategic plans, and the support he had immediately been given by his officers, he had awoken this morning with the powerful urge to avoid any fighting at all. When he had suggested a negotiation party to ride out and meet the Greeks, his officers had reacted with ill-concealed contempt, but he had insisted against all logic. Much to his own surprise, not to mention the astonishment of his officers, the Greek party had left their camp exactly at the same time. Now Dublyu realised how utterly silly and sentimental the whole idea of a negotiated peace had been. Yet he was puzzled by Tau's presence here: for some reason or other, the Greek general had also felt the need to ride out on a peace mission.

'Can I ask you something?' Dublyu suddenly said after what must have been a silence of nearly a full minute.

'Why am I here?'

'Exactly.'

'To be perfectly honest, Dublyu, I don't know. Somehow, I suddenly felt the need to try and settle all of this peacefully; against all my military instincts, I wanted to meet up with you and talk. I see now that I should never have given in to this whim. My reputation with my officers and troops may be irreparably damaged.'

'You probably won't believe me, but that's exactly what I felt. I hadn't planned this at all, whatever you may think.' Dublyu was keen to make it very clear to Tau that he wasn't here for any cowardly reasons, that he was as prepared to go on to the battlefield as his one-time friend.

'There's no need to persuade me of your courage, Dublyu,' Tau said with surprising gentleness. 'We must both have followed the same calling of the gods.'

'Is there any way out of this, you think?'

'I'm afraid we can't avoid a battle, my friend. Whatever made us come here has only served to make this more difficult for us personally, but there's no way we could possibly pull back.'

Reluctantly, Dublyu nodded. Of course, Tau was right. Without another word, both letters turned around, walked back to their bodyguards and gave the command to head back to the camp.

♣

That day's battle turned out not to be decisive after all. Dublyu's creative strategy proved effective up to a point, catching the Greeks off guard, but Tau was able to avoid defeat with an inspired move of the entire right flank of his army, effectively turning the Roman manoeuvre into an empty choreography of considerable beauty but little or no purpose. At the end of the day, the number of casualties on each side was sadly large, but neither side was able to claim victory.

General Dublyu was confused; he still didn't know what to make of the surreal events of the morning, when he and Tau had answered the same mysterious call. And with hindsight, it was impossible to see what purpose it had served. If the gods had been involved, they had certainly lost face, as the battle had gone ahead anyway. Not a single letter had been saved as a result of the little interlude. And the reputations of both generals had been at least dented, if not worse. The only positive element in that respect was the fact that the move had come from both sides simultaneously, so that neither side could be said to have acted any more cowardly than the other. Personally, Dublyu blamed himself: he shouldn't have allowed his thoughts to wander to his family. That had turned him soft and open to unmilitary thoughts. His love for his wife and children should not take away from his decisiveness on the battlefield, and he firmly intended not to let that happen again.

General Tau, too, blamed himself: how could he have been so stupid as to give in to a senseless idea like that? With all those years of experience behind him, he should have known better than to think sentimental thoughts. From now on, he would ban everything that could remind him of his family from his tent, and he would tell Zeta not to write to him anymore while he was away on a campaign. Her letters only distracted from military matters, and he wasn't going to allow that anymore. After all, the next battle was bound to be the decisive one.

♣

All over the Greek and Roman camps, letters of all ranks that had survived the battle were writing to their wives, sweethearts and mothers, telling them about how they were safe and sound, and how the day had started off so strangely, how their general had suddenly seemed so much like them: tired of fighting and the endless killing.

Rho and Jay – an impossible love

In the warm early evening air in Galaria, a small town in northern Greece, Rho made his way to the bridge across the river and its border post. The guards knew him well by now, and the crossing from Greek territory into Roman alphabet-controlled Macedonia was a mere formality nowadays anyway. Over the past few months, the young letter had made the crossing countless times, even though he had consciously kept it a secret from most of his family and friends. They wouldn't understand why he would voluntarily venture into foreign and hostile territory. The Greek and Roman alphabets were still officially at war, although an uneasy and unofficial peace had now held for over two years.

The bored border guards, who were near the end of their shift, did not even ask Rho for any pass, but just waved him through. They had seen him come and go regularly since last February, and had lost any interest in the possible reasons behind the handsome letter's visits to Roman territory. They had speculated in the beginning, of course, but as time went on, they had gradually stopped questioning Rho's claims that he was just crossing on business. On the other side of the bridge, the Roman guards at their post had come to view Rho's crossings with the same casual disinterest. What did they care why a silly young Greek letter wanted to come into Macedonia so often? As long as he didn't bring an army with him, they couldn't care less.

Rho's business in Macedonia was anything but businesslike: he was on a romantic quest. He had fallen in love with a Roman letter Jay he had glimpsed travelling through his town in a coach last February. He couldn't explain why the mere sight of her, however brief, had started a torrent of emotions in his Greek heart. He had simply known that, in spite of the impossibility of it all, he wanted to spend the rest of his life with this graceful letter, marry her and possibly even have little letters, whatever they might look like. It had been surprisingly easy to find out where she lived – an ink trader who had travelled between Roman and Greek territories all his life had come up with a good many details about Jay's family as soon as Rho had described the coach to him. 'Very high-class family, that, my lad,' he had said. 'Live in absolute luxury in Patanium just across the border, they do.'

Once Rho had crossed the river, it was only a half-hour walk to the outskirts of Patanium, where Jay and he had arranged to meet tonight. They had found a secluded spot on the edge of a cork oak wood, only a hundred yards from the road and about half a mile from the river, but well hidden from view. When Rho walked the last few yards through the dry grass, he called out in a whisper.

'Jay, kitten, are you there?'

No answer came, and Rho's heart sank, even though he knew he was early. He was always early, and only once had Jay already been waiting for him. Usually, he had to wait a while, and on two occasions, Jay had failed to show up at all, because she hadn't been able to get away from her family unnoticed. Rho sat down in the grass, with his back against a young tree, and smiled. In a little while, he would be near his lover again, and with any luck they would stay together until dawn. Jay's lovely features – the elegant curl of her head, the majestic downward sweep of her body – were on his mind most of the time anyway, but knowing that she would be here any minute now only heightened his awareness of her physical appearance. It was growing dark now; it was that magical hour when the sky is still full of light but hardly any of it reaches the ground anymore. Colours suffused the sky, highlighting the fringes of the clouds.

'Rho, tiger, are you there?'

The whisper of Jay's voice shook Rho out of his daydream. He was on his feet in a flash, ready to embrace his girl. The smile dropped from his face the moment he set eyes on Jay.

'What's the matter, kitten? Have you been crying?'

Jay did not answer, but started sobbing instead. Big tears welled up from her eyes and fell on Rho's wide shoulder. He held Jay close, and waited for the sobbing to subside.

'My brother has somehow found out we're seeing each other,' Jay managed to say after a while.

'But how could he know about us? Nobody knows!'

'I don't know, Rho, but he does. And I'm sure he's going to tell my father.' Jay burst into tears again.

Rho pulled her closer again, while all kinds of thoughts flashed through his mind. What would Jay's father do? Would he hurt her? Would he come after him? Was there any way for them to continue seeing one another, or was there really no future at all for them?

'I'm afraid, Rho.' Jay's voice trembled. 'My father will be furious when he hears I've been seeing a Greek letter. I'm afraid to go home.'

'Damn these Alphabet Wars! They've brought nothing but misery to ordinary letters. Who cares whether words are written one way or another? I love you, Jay, and I don't want to live without you.'

Jay's heart warmed in spite of her fear and sorrow. 'I love you so much, tiger,' she whispered. 'Nothing my father says or does can change that.'

'Can you stay here with me tonight? In the morning we'll decide what we'll do. I'm sure we'll find a way out of this.' Rho tried to sound confident, but he knew his faltering voice was at odds with what he was saying. Jay didn't say anything, and just kissed him lightly but with incredible tenderness.

♣

Gee was slightly disappointed with his father's reaction to the dramatic news. Where he had expected a violent rage, all he saw was controlled surprise. 'So your sister has acquired a Greek boyfriend, has she? We'll have to put a stop to that,' the old businessman said, quite calmly. Gee had only told his father because he was relishing the shock it would give him, and the outburst that was bound to follow. He didn't dislike his sister all that much, but he had always shown a ruthless streak, a tendency to enjoy discomfort or even pain in others. So he was put out, to say the least, when his provocation failed to produce the desired effect.

But for all his scheming and manipulation, Gee was not very good at reading his father's moods and feelings. Inside, the respected patriarch was seething; he only managed to retain his outward composure with enormous effort. He was a war veteran, had fought under General Dublyu for years, up until the unofficial truce about two years after that strange battle that had come to be known as the 'Negotiation Battle'. Even though it was almost four years ago now, Aey remembered that day as if it was yesterday. And he hadn't fought so long, seen so many of his fellow letters fall and lost part of his left leg himself to see his own daughter befriend a Greek letter, let alone be seduced by one, heaven forbid!

He would keep her at home for a while, lock her in her room if necessary, and arrange for the Greek good-for-nothing to be taught a lesson. It wouldn't be hard to find out who he was – not with the kind of contacts he could call on. The only tricky part was to keep all of this under wraps; he had no desire at all for the family reputation to be blackened by an unfortunate indiscretion like this. And first of all he would have to ensure that his son Gee kept his treacherous little trap shut. Although he had never shown it to anyone, he intensely disliked his scheming son.

'Gee,' he said, when his son was almost out of the room, 'come back here a minute, will you?'

Gee felt a chill creep down his limbs; his father's voice, though quite soft, had a threatening edge to it, and for once Gee didn't even think of finding an excuse to disobey him.

'Yes, father?' he wheedled.

'Close the door, son.'

In silence, Gee did as he was instructed.

'How did you find out about your sister's involvement with this Greek letter?'

Gee hesitated just a bit too long for his father's liking.

'Don't even think about lying to me, Gee!' Aey thundered. 'Don't beat about the bush; just tell me!'

Gee trembled, and his voice shook when he answered his father: 'One evening when she left the house, I followed her and saw her meet up with him. He's a Rho, and they must have been seeing each other for a while, because they have this hide-out near the Galaria road, and... and... they kissed.'

Aey only had to look at his son to indicate that he didn't want him to stop yet. Gee was glad not to have to endure the lash of his father's voice again; he swallowed and continued:

'They talked and cuddled and kissed for nearly three hours, and then the Greek boy walked back down the road towards the border. Honestly, father, that's all I know!'

Aey lowered his voice to no more than a whisper; it was clear, though, that he was in no mood to be contradicted. The threatening tone of his voice frightened Gee more than he had ever been in his entire life. 'Listen to me carefully, Gee, I'm only going to say this once. You will never again mention what you've seen to anyone, is that clear?'

Gee just nodded; he had lost all control over his voice, and his father, who in contrast to his son was very good at reading other letters' faces, knew he did not need to insist any further. 'You can go now,' he simply said. He then watched his son get to his feet unsteadily and walk out of the door. The old colonel then sat down at the table and sighed deeply. He was genuinely hurt by his daughter's lack of judgement. He just couldn't believe how she could have betrayed her own kind like that. Ever since she was born, he had instilled in her the true Roman values, or so he had always thought. Maybe the pain he felt was as much to do with the disappointment he felt in himself: he should have noticed long ago that Jay had stopped believing in the Roman way. A wave of indignation swept over him once more. How could she? A Greek letter, an enemy of the Roman alphabet! How could she feel anything but disgust for his kind? She needed to be saved from herself; not a moment was to be lost. He called his servant letter and instructed him to go and find Captain Tee at the barracks immediately, and to summon him to come to his superior at once.

♣

The eastern sky was just beginning to lose the inky blackness of the night when Rho woke with Jay's head on his shoulder and her limb pressing against his back. She had sobbed herself to sleep only a few hours earlier, and all Rho had been able to do was whisper sweet words to her. He lay very still; he didn't want to wake her yet, but wanted to think of something, some action or other they could undertake. If her brother had told her father about her love for him – and she was in no doubt at all about that – they would not have long before they'd have to act. The Colonel might well have sent out soldiers to their hiding place already. In spite of this realisation, Rho was strangely reluctant to wake Jay. He wanted nothing more than to lie here forever, with her head on his shoulder and her body trustingly close to his.

Rho suddenly heard a noise and instinctively sat up, making Jay wake up with a start. 'What…' she blurted out before Rho shushed her.

'I've heard something; sounds like a patrol has stopped on the road and is heading in this direction,' he whispered. 'We'll have to head for the river and escape that way; they're bound to find our hide-out.'

'I'll kill Gee! He must have told my father about our hide-out as well.' Jay trembled, not with fear but with rage. They both got up and set off towards the river, hiding in the high grass and moving as quietly as possible. Maybe the patrol would turn back when they found the hide-out empty. The fear of being discovered helped Jay concentrate on keeping her progress through the grass as unobtrusive as possible. Rho was in front of her, expertly negotiating his way to the river without a sound, and making it easy for Jay to just follow his lead. After a nerve-racking thirty minutes they reached the riverbank. They could see a small rowboat just upstream from where they had emerged from the grass and reeds. There was no sign of the patrol having followed them, and they looked at each other and headed for the boat.

It was only when Rho was pulling hard on the oars to get the boat away from the bank that Jay suddenly spoke. 'Where are we going?' she asked.

Rho realised that he had automatically assumed they would flee towards Greece, and felt shame at not having thought of the consequences. It would be nearly impossible for Jay to remain inconspicuous as soon as they crossed the border. The crossing itself might already prove tricky to say the least. 'I'm sorry, I really haven't thought this through, Jay,' he said.

'Where can we go?' The desperation and fear were obvious in her voice. 'We can't go anywhere, can we?'

'There must be something we can do', Rho said defiantly. 'You don't want to go back to your family, do you?'

Jay didn't know what to say, and just looked at Rho. He looked back at her, and tears filled his eyes, as the desperation of their situation began to sink in.

'A disguise', he said, 'you need a disguise. It should be possible to get you to look like an Iota. We only need to cover up your lower curl. Can you pull down your dress that far?'

'I don't really want to go to Greece, Rho.' Jay's voice was almost inaudible, but the look in her eyes carried the meaning of her words as clearly as if she had shouted them.

'We don't have much choice, kitten; it'll be much easier for me to organise some kind of cover when I'm home. Here on Roman territory, we'd both be fugitives, but in Greece at least I'm at home, and it'll be much harder for your father to find us. He can only send his patrols as far as the border and I doubt whether he has enough clout in Greece to have us traced.'

Although Jay was far from convinced that this plan would work, she saw that it did open up a possibility of staying with Rho, and that at least was something to look forward to. She hastily grabbed the hem of her dress, and started to tear the stitches. There were a good few inches there that would lengthen her dress almost to the ground. 'I think it'll be long enough, Rho,' she smiled. 'But how will I get across the border? I haven't got any papers on me.'

'If we can get to the other side of the river unnoticed, I think we can get to Galaria without being spotted. The border patrols have been scaled down over the past few months. We'll find a place for you to hide outside the town for a few days, while we decide what to do.' Rho felt very confident; they'd been able to outsmart the Colonel's patrol, hadn't they? The rest of the way to Galaria wouldn't be half as difficult to negotiate.

♣

Captain Tee shrank under the glare that the Colonel gave him even before the inevitable chewing out came. He was well aware of the fact that his patrol had been a miserable failure. Even though they had had fairly accurate information and had proceeded with due care, they had found the hiding place deserted, with no clues as to where the two youngsters had fled to. The march back to the Colonel's residence had been one of the most excruciatingly embarrassing of his entire career. Now he was facing his formidable superior, and he did not expect to get off lightly.

'You incompetent idiot!' Aey roared. 'You couldn't find an elephant if it was leaning against your crossbar. With all the information you had it should have been child's play to find them both and bring them back here. I have a good mind to have you court-martialled for dereliction of duty – you and your entire patrol'.

'Sir, I...,' Tee began, but the Colonel cut him off before he could even start apologising.

'I don't want to hear any of your pathetic excuses. You were given a simple mission, and you utterly failed to complete it. That's all there is to it. Get out of my sight, you miserable fool!' Aey's shouting could be heard all through the house, and Gee, who had just about regained his composure, sank back into the despair of one who knows the fear will never completely go away. He was past wishing that he had never followed his sister to discover her disgraceful secret. He only saw one possible way out of his misery: erasing himself. Only hours ago, he would have maintained that such thoughts were only for cowards and losers, but now he was finding the idea very attractive. Shredding himself was out of the question, though:

everyone with any sense knew it was the most painful method of all. No, he'd go for a solvent. Rumour had it that you only got a warm feeling all over before you dissolved into unconsciousness. He even knew where to get the solvent: his father kept some in his study.

Meanwhile, Aey's thoughts were not of his son, but of his daughter. In spite of his rage at Tee's failure to bring her back home, he wasn't so much angry with Jay as annoyed and disappointed. Actually, he was beginning to get quite worried, as it was obvious that his daughter had chosen to flee with this Greek letter rather than return home to her family. Where had he failed in his fatherly duties? He had only ever had the best intentions with Jay, had given her everything she wanted, within reason, and had loved her more than anyone or anything else in this world. The mere thought of his daughter rejecting that love caused him great pain.

Neither as a father, nor as an officer did he know what to do next. Most likely, Jay and her Greek friend – Aey could not bring himself to think of the Greek letter as her lover – would have fled to Greece. If they had succeeded in crossing the border, there was very little he could do to track them down. He might have ordered a couple of covert operations across the border in the past couple of years, but those had been relatively simple eliminations of known double agents whose exact location was known. Moreover, the chance of the Greeks mounting any kind of action in reaction to the operations – even if they were aware of them – was almost nonexistent, as double agents weren't exactly the most trusted or appreciated elements. But pursuing a couple of ordinary letters, one of them a Greek letter, heaven knew how far into Greece, was not just suicidal, but an open challenge to restart the Alphabet Wars in earnest. It just could not be done. He could only hope that the impossibility of continuing to hide as a Roman letter in enemy territory would force Jay to return home eventually.

♣

Jay was half asleep in the drowsy heat and gloomy semi-darkness of the barn where Rho had brought her to hide. There was precious little else to do apart from worrying, and over the past couple of days she had found that she had become rather fatalistic about any possible future Rho and she might have. There was no point in being afraid of being discovered – in fact fear would probably just heighten the chances of being found out. For the first half day or so, Jay had worked herself into a frenzy, going over all kinds of scenarios: what if her father managed to have her captured and brought back home? What if something happened to Rho and she was left on her own in Greece? What if someone else happened to discover her hiding place? Then, quite suddenly, a kind of feeling of calm, even apathy, had rolled over her, giving way to sleepiness. From that moment onwards, she had slept or dozed most of the time, except for the moments that Rho came to visit her.

He had found the barn within hours of them crossing the border, and since then had been frantically trying to find a way of getting her to permanent safety. He had been to the barn twice to keep her up to speed with his efforts, but on his last visit had been visibly discouraged as he was running out of ideas. With a total lack of emotion, Jay was beginning to consider the idea that it might prove impossible for them to have a future together; that she would just have to return home and accept whatever her father might have planned for her.

A sound outside the barn made Jay sit up, her apathy instantly turning to fear again. Was this the moment that she was to be discovered? She held her breath. The barn door opened slowly, and a shadow fell across the harsh sunlight streaming through the open door. A letter came into the barn, and for a moment Jay, blinded by the light, could not tell who it was. Then the familiar tones of Rho's voice sounded out: 'It's only me!'

The two letters hugged and kissed, and sat down on one of the many bales of hay in the barn. Jay could feel that Rho was excited; she didn't get the chance to ask him what it was, though, as he blurted out: 'I think I've found a solution, Jay! We can be together for the rest of our lives, get married, have children!'

Jay's spirits rose from the torpor of the past days, and her eyes brightened as she looked at Rho with a dazzling smile. When he saw the expectation in Jay's face, Rho faltered slightly. He hesitated for a moment, and then said: 'But we would have to stay in Greece, I'm afraid, and there's another sacrifice you would have to make.'

The words hung heavily between them as Jay's smile slowly disappeared; her head sank slowly. Then she looked at Rho again, whispering: 'If it means we can be together, I'd do anything.'

Rho took a deep breath, and then came out with his plan. It had come to him when he was beginning to despair about how utterly impossible it seemed for a Roman and a Greek letter to be together. The thought of why he couldn't be Roman or Jay couldn't be Greek suddenly led him to the glaringly obvious: it *was* possible for Jay to be turned into a Greek letter! She had disguised herself as an Iota when they were fleeing Macedonia; if she was willing to undergo calligraphic surgery, she could effectively become an Iota, and their future would be secure. They would only have to find a calligrapher that was prepared to be discreet, and that shouldn't be too difficult: discretion was an essential part of their profession.

Jay was silent for a while, but just when Rho was starting to think she would refuse, she turned to him, smiled and kissed him. 'You'd better start getting used to calling me Iota, then,' she said.

A Day in the Life of a Soldier of the Imperial Roman Army

'This ink is so watered down a dot couldn't live on it,' Kay muttered, 'and we're supposed to march on it day in day out?' He swirled the black, watery daily ration around in his tin cup and peered into it suspiciously before sniffing it for the fourth time since he had collected it from the camp kitchen.

'I'll drink it if you don't want it,' his sergeant, Eitch, volunteered. 'I've seen much worse over the past few years. I remember the...'

'The Chinese campaign, I know,' Kay sighed. 'You've only told me that about a dozen times. You fought on no more than three drops of pure ink a day, or is it down to two in the latest version?'

'Well, it was much worse than anything you've ever seen, I'll tell you that much for free,' Eitch snapped.

'All right, I'm sorry, no need to get all worked up about it, sarge; it's just that I've heard the stories before, right?' Kay said, trying to calm Eitch. He knew how excited he could become about his experiences during the Eastern Campaigns. Even though the stories could sometimes become very repetitive, Kay had learnt quite a lot about the Eastern Campaigns and the ensuing Alphabet Wars in the eight months since he had joined the army and had been assigned to the 14th. Kay had to admit that he was fascinated by sergeant Eitch's accounts of how he had fought alongside the Greeks against the Chinese character army. He imagined what it must have been like to face such strange creatures, with their multiple strokes, far more complex than any Roman letter. He had seen images of them, of course, but he'd never met one in real life. It was only soldiers like Eitch who had actually fought them, that could claim to really know what the Chinese looked like. And there weren't too many of them around anymore; after all, the Eastern Campaigns had finished about twenty years before Kay had even joined the army. Eitch was one of those perennial sergeants you find in any army, gruff but warm-hearted, a superior but at the same time a friend.

The Roman Army was at war with the Phoenicians right now, and the 14th Regiment, part of the 2nd Army, was marching on the city of Sarepta after having crossed the Mediterranean. Alongside the Roman Army, the Greek 3rd Army was also part of the massive assault on the Phoenician heartland. The alliance between the Greek and Roman alphabets in these so-called Alphabet Wars had held for nearly ten years now, in spite of occasional tension. It was a bit of an uncomfortable and strange situation, such an alliance, as alphabets essentially were always after a monopoly. You can't compromise between two writing systems – it's one or the other. But history was peppered with examples of usually short-term alliances between alphabets, generally in order to defeat a common enemy. The Phoenician alphabet was on its last legs, and the Roman-Greek alliance was generally expected to dissolve once the Phoenicians were defeated. Even now, there was only contact between the Greek and Roman army commanders; the letters themselves only occasionally caught glimpses of the foreign regiments on the march. Kay had never even seen a Greek letter up close, but everyone knew that they were more similar to Roman letters than any others.

'Were the Chinese characters good fighters, sarge?' Kay asked, trying to get Eitch in a good mood again.

'Never you mind about the Chinese, son,' Eitch answered. 'You'd better finish your ink and pack up. We'll be marching out in twenty minutes.' He raised his voice to his characteristic bellow, trying to find the company's bugler: 'Wye, you lazy devil, where are you? Get your bugle over here this minute!'

Kay's company was a mixed one in a mixed regiment, with all kinds of letters, but all of them Times New Roman, the soldiers 10 point, NCOs 12 point and officers 14 point. Most regiments were single-font, and some companies were single-character, but only few regiments were single-font-single-character. Those were the crack troops, and they had a fearsome reputation. It was every soldier's dream to distinguish themselves to such an extent that they were transferred to such a regiment. Sergeant Eitch tended to be very dismissive (and very rude, Kay thought) about the merits of those crack regiments. 'Diversity is worth more than uniformity on the battlefield,' he would say. Kay supposed he was just jealous, and disappointed that he had never made it into an SFSC regiment.

♣

They had been marching for over four hours now without any break at all, and the fatigue was beginning to tell. The heat of the sun didn't help, either, and even Sergeant Eitch seemed to be tiring somewhat. Then, fortunately, the command to halt was shouted down the line. The soldiers just flung down their packs and flopped down on the ground. Eitch, who was normally a stickler for drill discipline, didn't bother to reprimand them. He knew they had been kept on their feet for far too long, and shouting at them now would have no effect whatsoever.

'I remember...,' he began, and some of the letters groaned, more out of habit than anything else. The sergeant could be tiresome at times with his endless stories of the Eastern Campaigns, but mostly the soldiers actually enjoyed his tall tales. 'I remember,' Eitch repeated, 'the time when we were marching through Rajasthan on the way to China and they kept us on our feet all day long without a break. And it was hotter than it is today, I can tell you, much hotter. Most of Rajasthan is desert anyway, so you can imagine the state we were in when we finally stopped at night. So don't you go thinking you've had a hard time this morning. It's only just gone noon and we've already stopped.'

'Was that right at the start of the Alphabet Wars, sarge?' one of the newest recruits asked.

'Give me strength!' Eitch sighed in mock despair. 'Don't they teach you youngsters any history anymore? The Alphabet Wars are being fought in Europe and around the Mediterranean, Private Dee, and they only started eighteen years ago! How can you ever be expected to fight well if you don't even have a clue what war you're fighting in?' He sighed again, but that was for the soldiers' benefit; actually, Eitch was always grateful for an opportunity to tell the young letters about the history of the Alphabet Wars. The soldiers felt one of the sergeant's lectures coming on, and settled back against their backpacks.

'All right then,' Eitch said, 'the Alphabet Wars, as you should all know...' He looked around as the letters, exhausted but happy enough to be sitting down, all looked at him expectantly. 'The Alphabet Wars are all about getting our Roman alphabet the dominant position it deserves in Europe and along the Mediterranean shores.' He hesitated for a moment, grinned and said: 'Giving our great allies the Greeks their rightful position as well, of course,' adding, in a much lower voice, 'as long as we need them.' A few of the older soldiers, who could remember the time before the Roman-Greek alliance, sniggered, drawing puzzled looks from the younger recruits. 'All right, pay attention,' Eitch said, 'so the Alphabet Wars are basically a European conflict. But before these Alphabet Wars, the much bigger fight was between the different writing systems: ideographic, cuneiform, hieroglyphic, syllabic and alphabetic.' He paused, knowing that most of the letters would not understand the technical terms. He enjoyed the puzzled looks they were giving each other, waiting to see who'd pluck up the courage to admit to their ignorance.

It was Kay who spoke up. 'Sorry, Sarge, but what does ideographic mean?' This was the signal for others to voice their confusion. 'Yeah, and what's cunning-form?' 'Are hired glyphs like mercenaries?' 'What the fuck is a silly bick?'

'All right already!' Eitch shouted. 'First of all, private Eph, I've bloody well told you before that swearing is a sergeant's privilege; secondly, if you'd all shut your traps a moment, I could tell you what those things mean.' He was secretly enjoying himself; he always thought he would have made a good teacher if he hadn't been drafted into the army. 'Let's tackle this systematically. You know that our way of writing, the alphabetic way, basically uses a letter for every sound, and the letters are combined to form words, with a meaning, right?' All around him, the letters were nodding. 'Well, in the ideographic system, characters, their equivalent to letters, stand for a meaning, or part of a meaning. So to make things really simple, you might even say that a character is almost like a word. Got that?' The nods of the letters were a bit more uncertain, but Eitch got the impression that most of them were still with him. 'So it's a different system of writing down language. Cuneiform and hieroglyphic systems were originally drawings that later changed into more stylised symbols that stand for words or meanings. Actually, all three of them, ideographic, cuneiform and hieroglyphic, were similar in concept, using simplified pictures to write down words, if you really want the version for dummies.' Around him, heads started nodding again; the last, simple explanation made sense.

'Only the ideographic system still exists,' Eitch continued. 'The other two were defeated and are hardly used anymore, which leaves the syllabic writing system that uses one symbol, one letter if you want, not for one sound, but for one syllable. All right, any more questions?'

Private Dee hesitantly piped up again: 'But weren't they all defeated in... eh... before the Alphabet Wars then?'

'No, Private Dee for dummy, the ideographic and syllabic systems are very much alive and kicking. The Eastern Campaigns, which is when the alphabets fought a number of the other systems, were not fought to the end. The grand coalition between the alphabetic systems broke up, and strong though our Roman alphabet is, we couldn't fight the other systems on our own, so we retreated. But it wouldn't surprise me at all if there were more wars between the different systems before too long.'

Some of the younger letters were looking at their sergeant with something near adoration – they knew him as a good storyteller, but they'd never heard him explain politics in such detail, and with obvious expertise. So he isn't just a simple ignorant fighter after all, you could almost hear them think. The soldiers who had been with Eitch a bit longer already knew that, but it never ceased to surprise them how well he could normally hide it.

'Now if you'll leave me in peace for a moment, I'll go and see whether I can find out what the rest of the day has in store for us,' sergeant Eitch said gruffly, effortlessly reverting to his everyday character. 'In the meantime, smarten up! Some of you look as if you've been in the wars.' There was a good deal of good-humoured laughing and sniggering, and Eitch knew that he'd done his duty: the letters had forgotten how tired and downhearted they'd been.

Kay looked around him as he stood up and straightened his uniform. He hadn't been as surprised by the sergeant's display of knowledge as most of his companions, but then he had been talking to Eitch quite a lot over the past weeks. It seemed as if the sergeant had taken a shine to him, and Kay was also beginning to appreciate him more and more. It had been clear on a few earlier occasions that there was more to the sergeant than you'd think if you took him at face value.

'Well, it looks as if we might be fighting tomorrow,' Eitch said in a low voice, leaning over to Kay. The young letter was taken aback, and at first thought he hadn't understood his sergeant correctly. After all, when Sergeant Eitch had come back to his company, he had been all smiles, bearing the good news that they'd be stopping for two hours, and that they'd all be getting an extra half pint of ink for lunch, to compensate for the long march.

'What?' said Kay, and his puzzled look made Eitch smile again.

'I said, we might be in for a fight tomorrow,' the sergeant said again. 'You know, fighting, against the Phoenicians,' he added sarcastically, still keeping his voice down.

'B...but....,' Kay stammered, 'you seemed so upbeat when you came back with the orders.'

'Yes,' Eitch teased, 'so what?'

'And they're letting us rest after the long march of this morning, and we're getting... extra rations...,' Kay said, beginning to realise the warped logic of the situation.

'Exactly,' Eitch nodded slowly, 'so unless the big brass have suddenly developed a compassionate streak, which frankly isn't very likely, it just means they want us well rested and fed to face the Phoenician army, right?'

Kay just nodded, and suddenly felt exhausted again. He'd only been in two full-scale battles up to now, and he hadn't liked them one bit. All the noise, the screaming of maimed letters, the severed limbs, half-erased bodies, and the ink, all that spilt ink! Not the fresh, sweet-smelling ink, straight from the bottle, that sustained them all, but the thicker, darker, life-carrying stuff that oozed from the letters and limbs as they lay dying; the ink that covered you during the course of the battle, no matter how much you tried to avoid it, and clung to you in dirty streaks and congealed blobs; the ink that you had to scrape off laboriously after the fighting had stopped. Days later, he had still discovered small dried patches of ink in the creases of his own limbs. He shivered. In spite of all the bravado that he displayed to his companions, he desperately did not want to be in another battle. It had really taken him by surprise that the relief of having survived was utterly overshadowed by the horror of the slaughter on the battlefield.

In a surprisingly compassionate voice, Eitch reassured Kay: 'I could be wrong, of course. After all, the plan was to march on to Sarepta and lay siege to the city. And even if a Phoenician force has been spotted and our commanders wanted to fight before we come to Sarepta, it's far from certain that the Phoenicians would share that desire. They might just want to flee, or simply surrender; they know they haven't got a chance in hell of winning a fight.'

'Thanks, sarge,' Kay said, forcing a smile. 'It's just that I'm not really keen on another battle, you know.'

'Nobody in their right mind is, lad. But being all gloomy about it won't help, either; better think positive. That rubs off on the others even more than pessimism, believe you me!'

In Kay's already high opinion of the sergeant, he had just gone up another notch. He really had all their best interests at heart, and his smiles earlier had not been deception, but a matter of buoying their spirits in preparation for what might come. And in spite of Eitch's frankness with him, Kay himself could feel that it was working: if he had to face another battle, he'd much rather do it with sergeant Eitch and the rest of his company than with any of the crack regiments. If the Phoenicians thought they even had the merest whisker of a chance against the 14th, they were very much mistaken.

Sooner than they'd all hoped, the order to march on came, and it was back to the dull drudgery, the mind-numbing endless thumping of thousands of limbs. It was either a matter of switching off completely, Kay had learnt, or focusing on something else entirely. If you allowed yourself to actually think of the marching itself, it became sheer torture after half an hour. He had become quite adept by now at conjuring up entire episodes from his childhood, and over the past few months had even surprised himself that he was able to clearly remember as far back as the beginning of his schooling, when he was a mere four-pointer. He was just in the middle of a fabulously entertaining school outing with one of his favourite teachers when he suddenly realised that the company had come to a halt. Like an automaton, he had stopped with the rest of them when Eitch had shouted out the command.

The sun was still high in the sky, though, so they couldn't have been marching for more than two hours. When the order came to pitch the tents, Kay looked at Eitch, realising the only possible reason for this early stop was that they'd be facing battle tomorrow morning. Eitch just looked back at him, and didn't even have to signal that he knew that Kay had understood.

It was over dinner – everybody was in a good mood because of the unhoped-for portion of ink after the already generous lunch rations, except for Kay, who couldn't help thinking about the reason for this abundance of food – that Sergeant Eitch relayed the news to the company. Again, Kay could only admire the insight of the old campaigner. He presented the upcoming battle as an unexpected opportunity for them to prove that their training had not been in vain, appealed to the comradeship they all felt for one another, and even jokingly referred to their loyalty to himself as their sergeant. The upbeat mood Eitch managed to convey all through his speech unavoidably filled the soldiers with enthusiasm; they had no space left in their minds for fear after the pep-talk had charged them to the brim with positive feelings of confidence and duty. The fact that they had forgotten all about the much more useful logic of self-preservation did not, for the moment, occur to them. Even Kay felt a rush of expectation, and when he fell asleep that night, it was with the warm glow of self-confidence inside.

♣

It was highly unusual for Kay to be woken by reveille. Most days, he woke at least half an hour before the shrill military wake-up call. He had slept soundly and peacefully in spite of the impending battle, thanks to Eitch's inspiring words. But now the cold reality began to seep back in, and he hoped the sergeant would be his confident self this morning and bolster his troops' courage.

As if on cue, the tent flaps opened to reveal a cheerful Sergeant Eitch. 'Come on, you sleeping beauties, rise and shine. We don't want to keep those poor Phoenician letters waiting, do we?' Unlikely though it might be, Kay felt his misgivings subside, just hearing Eitch's jocular tone of voice.

'They'll really be "poor Phoenicians" once we've finished with them, Sarge,' he said, making his voice as cheerful as he could manage.

'That's the spirit, lad,' Eitch said while he was already on his way out to the next tent. 'The bastards won't know what hit them!'

There wasn't any time to go back to being afraid during the next hour or so, as they rushed from sorting out their own stuff to putting on the battle gear, from preparing the artillery carts to sharpening their swords and distributing solvent grenades. If anything, there was a certain eagerness in the air, an optimistic expectancy. So every letter in the Roman army was almost relieved when the order to fall in came, and all the companies of the 14th regiment and all the other regiments of the 2nd Army lined up, ready for action.

When Kay looked around him, he could see the banners of the other regiments of the 2nd Army, and beyond them the less familiar ones of the Greek 3rd Army, and was impressed by the size of the force. Because they were on a slight slope, he got a better idea of the sheer number of letters involved than he had been able to on previous occasions. He had been told there were 28,000 letters in the 2nd Army, and 21,000 in the Greek 3rd Army, and even though he could not make out individuals much beyond his own regiment, he felt the presence of each of those thousands of letters as if they were all standing next to him. The feeling was one of overwhelming power, of trust in his fellow soldiers. There was no way this army was going to lose the battle – that was just unthinkable.

At the bottom of the slope he could just about make out the enemy army – a shimmering, anonymous mass that seemed smaller than the Roman-Greek force. Eitch had told them yesterday night that they would be outnumbering the Phoenicians two to one, and if anything Kay thought that might be overestimating the size of the enemy. He almost felt pity for the letters down there, facing the might of the combined forces of the Roman Imperial Army and the Greek troops. Would they be scared, or would their own sergeants have given them the courage and confidence that Eitch had instilled in his company? Was there a Kay among the Phoenician letters, someone with the same mix of bravado, fear, apprehension, disgust, mindless optimism, confidence and fatalistic apathy that he felt? Kay shivered and tried to clear his mind – he didn't want to think of the enemy as individual letters with similar feelings to his own. That made fighting them wrong, an evil thing to do.

Sergeant Eitch walked along the line of soldiers, and when he passed Kay, stopped and faced the young soldier. 'Don't think too much, Private Kay,' he said. 'Brooding's never done anyone any good, especially before a battle.' He turned and walked on.

Kay was grateful for the interruption, and once more marvelled at the insight and sensitivity of his sergeant. It was as if the old letter could read his mind. The simple but timely words allowed him to focus his mind on the battle again, rather than waste his energy speculating about some imaginary counterpart in the Phoenician army. When he looked down the slope again, he could see movement in the first ranks of the Greek army, which had been positioned in front of the Roman troops, and at the same time he heard the distant sounds of bugles. The battle had started, and the excitement all around him mounted. It would be a while before their own company would start moving, though.

When eventually the signal to move forward came, they could see that the Phoenician army, or what was left of it, was already retreating. No, not retreating – that was too deliberate a word for the chaotic scattering of letters away from the battle lines. Behind Kay's company, he could hear commands to move around the bulk of the Roman army, undoubtedly an attempt to cut off the path of the fleeing Phoenicians. While the company was still marching towards the front line, Kay could see how the little that was left of the Phoenician forces was now really being slaughtered. Meanwhile, the fleeing letters were running into Roman soldiers cutting off their path, and some turned back towards the front. Annihilation was facing them whichever way they ran, and Kay simply stopped looking. He knew now that today he would not have to worry about being covered in ink or about survival. Yet somehow the thought could not lift his spirits; he let his mind go blank and unthinkingly followed the order to halt when it came.

The Reluctant Hero

Whenever Raw Ruua thought back to that fateful day, he'd feel an uncomfortable but not entirely unpleasant mixture of pride, regret and wistfulness. Pride because he had overcome what he had always considered a basically cowardly character; regret, because he hadn't been able to do more with his newfound courage; and wistfulness for the relatively carefree existence he had led up to then. It all seemed such a long time ago, though in reality the events that had so thoroughly changed his life had only taken place about three years earlier.

As he leant back, knowing that the hard decisions for the day had been taken, he allowed himself the luxury of smugness. As always, it was the gilt-framed parchment with the personal words of gratitude from the Thai King Haw Heep that brought on this uncharacteristic moment of self-indulgence. Not many letters could claim that their King knew them personally, let alone had written a personal message to them. So, Raw Ruua's reasoning went, if the King was so complimentary of him, he might be allowed to let pride outweigh the other feelings. After all, it was he, a lowly letter, and not one of those highly regarded, big Kaw Kai bodyguards who had saved the King's life. Yet just thinking of how he had been able to throw that Chinese assassin off balance just as she was shooting that vicious eraser-tipped arrow triggered the persistent regret that he had lacked the necessary courage to prevent her from annihilating the Princess Chaw Ching with that solvent grenade. A braver letter would either have knocked the assassin out, or at least have prevented him from throwing the grenade.

Raw Ruua had got his prestigious job as private secretary to the Governor of Phrae as a reward for his actions, but not a day went by when he didn't speculate what his reward would have been if he had also saved the Princess's life. He might well have become the King's private secretary!

A discreet knock on the door of his office saved him from further fruitless speculation. 'Come!' he said. His own secretary Sara Ah, a pretty and diligent young letter, came into the office. Raw Ruua couldn't deny he hadn't had fantasies about Sara Ah; to his credit, though, he had never let them get beyond the fantasy stage.

'I'm so sorry to disturb you, Khun Raw,' the girl trilled, in a voice not much above a whisper, 'but that journalist from Sawatdee Magazine has arrived. Shall I tell her to wait until you call her in?' As always, Sara Ah managed to convey both politeness and efficiency in her words and comportment. Raw Ruua just couldn't stop himself from thinking of her as Sexy Ah rather than Sara Ah. One of these days it would surely slip out when he wasn't concentrating.

'No need for her to wait, Khun Ah, she can come in straight away,' he smiled.

'As you wish, Khun Raw,' the young secretary said, bowing slightly.

Raw Ruua had dreaded the interview from the moment he had agreed to it, after masked but unmistakable pressure from the Governor. With the upcoming celebrations for the 25th anniversary of the King's coronation, the story of the failed assassination attempt three years ago was getting renewed interest in the press. Raw Ruua had gone over the whole episode in his own mind over and over again, had tried to think of all the possible questions he might be asked and the answers he should give. His wife Naw Nu had despaired of his insecurity and even become really angry at one point. Her uncharacteristic outburst had been the sign for him to realise that he was blowing the upcoming interview out of all proportion, and he had apologised for his behaviour. Yet he was still very nervous now that the moment had come.

The letter entering his office a few moments later was a middle-aged twelve-point sans serif font. With predictable efficiency, she only needed a moment to set the tone: it was going to be a no-nonsense interview. 'Good afternoon, Khun

Raw, I am Ngaw Ngu from Sawatdee Magazine. I made an appointment with you for an interview today.'

If anything, Raw Ruua was put at ease by the briskness of the journalist. 'Good afternoon, Khun Ngaw, please take a seat,' he said, getting out of his chair and indicating the chair on the other side of his desk. Once more, he promised himself that he would not allow himself to be unsettled by whatever questions she might throw at him.

'Would you mind if we started straight away, Khun Raw? I'm afraid I'm not one for drawn-out introductions or warm-up questions,' the journalist said in the clipped tones of someone who is used to getting her own way.

'Fine by me,' the Governor's secretary replied, feeling strangely reassured by the journalist's attitude that might well be interpreted as slightly hostile. It was the decisiveness of her words that instilled a similar lack of hesitation in him.

The first question was more than enough, though, to shatter Raw Ruua's confidence. 'In retrospect, Khun Raw, do you ever regret you were not able to save the Princess Chaw Ching's life as well as His Majesty the King's?' the interviewer asked, with no hint of either sympathy or malevolence.

There was an uncomfortable silence for a few seconds – although it seemed more like a lifetime for Raw Ruua. All manner of thoughts and scenarios flashed through his mind. It was unavoidable that someone would eventually expose him for the coward he was, and he might as well own up and beg for mercy straight away; what was this journalist's hidden agenda – was she actually working for the Chinese? He would undoubtedly lose his job as well as any respect – maybe he should start packing his things right now; the question was only intended to allow him to show his humility, not to humiliate him; who did this serpent of a journalist think she was, attacking a decorated hero? Every additional moment of silence would only show him to be more of a coward than he already was.

It was that last realisation which spurred him on to say something. 'Erm,' he started, 'it was of course an enormous loss for the entire nation that the Princess Royal was wiped out by the solvent grenade thrown by the Chinese assassin, but we should also be grateful that a powerful weapon like that did not make many more victims.' There, that would do as a basic defence. He was actually quite pleased with his response, and started to gain a bit of confidence.

'I'm sorry if my question implied any criticism, Khun Raw,' Ngaw Ngu said with surprising deference. It almost seemed as if she had been unsettled as much as her interviewee by the opening question. 'His Majesty himself has always said how grateful he is that there were not many more casualties. I only wanted our readers to get an insight into the feelings of the letter who saved the King.'

By now, Raw Ruua had regained his composure, and also knew that he didn't need to be afraid of this journalist. There wasn't any trace of irony in her reaction – she sounded positively apologetic. He got the feeling that if he played this well, he could determine himself exactly which way this interview would go.

'Thank you, Khun Ngaw, I appreciate your clarification. I think it's only to be expected that any letter would feel great sadness and regret at not being able to save the Princess Royal. I can honestly say that it was His Majesty King Haw Heep's kind words to me, on a number of occasions after the assassin's attack, that have allowed me to come to terms with this.' He hoped he wasn't overdoing it; after all, he had only met the King three times afterwards, and had only really spoken at any length with him on one occasion. But he could sense in the reaction of the journalist that this had been the right way to respond. She was eagerly writing down this combination of humility and praise for the monarch.

'I wonder if you could now describe the attack itself, Khun Raw. I realise that the event was widely covered in the press three years ago, but I am sure that our readers would like to be reminded, and that you may even be able to give a better account now that you have overcome the shock you must have felt back then.' It was a carefully phrased question, cleverly anticipating and rebutting any kind of protest. He would have to remain very alert all through the interview if he didn't want to be tricked into revealing something that could be used against him. At the same time, he was glad that the inevitable open question had come so early in the interview; this was the part he had been able to prepare carefully, and he was eager to give his account of the events that had made him into the letter he was now.

'As your readers will probably remember, everything happened during a visit of the Royal Family to Phrae for the celebrations of the 1,000[th] anniversary of the foundation of the city by the then King Taw Tahn. His Majesty the King, Her Majesty the Queen and Her Royal Highness the Princess Royal were attending a reception at the Governor's Residence. You can imagine the importance of such an event for Phrae and all its inhabitants, and the Governor had spared no expense to ensure that the Royal visit would be a memorable and enjoyable event.'

At that point, the journalist interrupted him: 'How did you come to be at the reception, Khun Raw?'

Raw Ruua's reaction sounded more aggressive than he intended it to be: 'I was coming to that, Khun Ngaw; I think the readers also deserve to see the larger setting.' He could see the journalist beginning to flush, which in turn made him realise he had been unnecessarily rude. He flushed himself, and stumbled, 'I mean, I... erm... if you don't mind... erm... I really was just about to...'

He checked himself, took a deep breath and continued his story with as much dignity as he could muster. 'The reception was to be one of the high points of the official part of the visit, and the Governor had hired the best caterers in the city. I happened to be working part-time for that catering firm; I was a student back then, in my final year at university. And so I found myself handing round crystal tumblers of the finest ink in the big hall of the Governor's Residence. I remember feeling very privileged and slightly overawed at being in the same room with the Royal Family and concentrating hard on my job. It was difficult not to constantly stare at the Royal visitors but to circulate and make sure everyone had a full glass. Earlier, His Majesty had made a fine speech on the importance of traditions and the continuing threat of the Chinese. It was the height of the so-called Dry War back then: there had been no actual fighting since the horrible Battle of Chiang Saen between the combined forces of the Thai, Burmese and Lanna alphabets and the

Chinese ideograms, and the ensuing cease-fire had held for nine years, but there was an awful lot of tension, and everybody feared that a resumption of hostilities was imminent. His Majesty had ended his speech with a call for constant vigilance. I suppose in the light of what happened later that was quite ironic. I was very much aware of the bodyguards and other security letters – there must have been about thirty of them, all big Kaw Kais and Taw Taos, and I was shocked to see that some of them were drinking and chatting.'

The question was to be expected, of course, and Raw Ruua could have kicked himself for the indiscreet comment he had made. 'Are you saying that the attack could have been prevented altogether if the guards had been more alert?' The last thing he wanted was to put the blame on the guards and to depict himself as the hero.

'No, please don't misunderstand me; I'm sure professionals like them are used to situations in which they have to blend in. After all, they don't want to constantly frighten everyone – letters should be able to feel at ease and enjoy themselves at a reception. Moreover, the assassin was brilliantly disguised; remember, we didn't know then that the Chinese had developed this pencil that is almost indistinguishable from black ink. It was the first time such a disguise was ever discovered. So, no, I don't think the attack could have been prevented.'

He paused, trying to gauge the effect of his attempt at damage control. The journalist's expression was difficult to read, but her words reassured him: 'Please do go on with your story, Khun Raw; I didn't want to interrupt you.'

Raw Ruua breathed a silent sigh of relief; he'd most probably got away with that slip-up. Now he could just get back to the story he had prepared.

'What happened next is much to do with coincidence – call it fate if you want. When the assassin took out her weapon, I was just heading for her, as I had noticed she wasn't holding a glass. Then I realised that she was holding a bow and raising it in the direction of His Majesty. I know it may sound terribly corny, but the recollection that I have of the events that followed is that everything happened in slow motion. I can see the string of the bow being pulled backwards by what I still thought to be a Thai letter, and then my tray, almost full with tumblers of black and dark blue ink slowly being propelled towards the assassin. When the tray hit her she dropped the arrow and lost her balance; while she staggered, the ink dripped all over her, revealing her true strokes under the disguise. It was then that not only I, but also the letters immediately around her, realised that she was a Chinese ideogram. I became aware of a roar of panic gradually spreading through the hall, and at that point things seemed to speed up to normal again.'

It was truly the way he remembered it – apart from one thing. He had left out what had seemed his endless hesitation and the turmoil in his mind when he had seen the bow. The internal fight between his inborn cowardice and fear on the one hand and an unfamiliar mix of other emotions – a sense of duty, an instinct to prevent evil from taking its course, even pride in having discovered what the professionals had failed to see – on the other hand had seemed to go on forever. He still didn't know exactly what it was that had made him decide to act by throwing his tray at the assassin. That was again where the story he had just told was the complete truth. It was as if he had just observed the tray sailing away from him. In a way, he wasn't even sure he was glad that he had acted. Surely, his life would have been simpler if he had just pretended he hadn't seen anything, if he hadn't done anything at all? He wouldn't have to go through the agony of this interview, for one.

He became aware of the slightly puzzled stare of Ngaw Ngu, who was no doubt wondering why he had suddenly stopped talking. This was the point at which the story was really coming to its climax, and she would not have anticipated him pausing now.

'I'm sorry,' he said quickly, 'the memory is still quite strong, and reliving it is not easy.' Inwardly, he cursed himself for letting his attention wander. He could already imagine which form this short pause in his story would take in the article; probably something along the lines of "overcome by emotions" or even "powerful memories bringing the hero close to tears" or some such nonsense. It would, after all, be a so-called 'alphabetic-interest article'.

He resumed his story before a further pause might lead to an unexpected question. 'Things really became confused at that moment; letters began to scream, some diving for cover, some rushing towards the exit, and at least a dozen bodyguards came running towards the assassin. Amid this bedlam, the Royal Family, as was to be expected of such dignified letters, remained calm, and showed no signs at all of panic. I saw the assassin reach inside her cape and produce a small object, like an oversized egg I remember thinking. If I had been in the army, I would no doubt have recognised it as a solvent grenade and I might have acted just in time. I was still marginally closer to the Chinese ideogram than the first of the onrushing bodyguards. The murderous villain threw the grenade towards the Royal Family, undoubtedly intending to hit His Majesty the King, but she didn't have the time to aim carefully, and the grenade hit the floor and exploded so close to the Her Royal Highness the Princess Royal that she dissolved almost instantly. By that time, two of the King's personal bodyguards had just reached him, shielding him from the blast. One was also dissolved instantly, and another was so gravely wounded that he succumbed to his injuries later. As you know, His Majesty himself was unhurt, as was the Queen, who was further away from the grenade.'

'And what were you doing in the meantime, Khun Raw?' the journalist asked, noticing that he had reached the end of his story. Obviously she would have noticed that he had prepared the whole thing – but then, who wouldn't have? And it wasn't as if this was the first time he was asked to tell the story; he must have told it hundreds of times by now. Almost every letter he had met since then had wanted to hear it; so much so that Raw Ruua had begun to avoid going to places or events where he was likely to run into too many letters.

'I was just standing there doing nothing, really. The bodyguards had already wrestled the assassin to the ground, and, frankly, I think I was in shock. I had never seen a Chinese ideogram in real life, and to tell you the truth I was still surprised at myself for my earlier reaction.' No, you're drawing attention to yourself now, he thought; too many references to the fact that you're telling the truth, and that makes it implausible.

It was as if the journalist had heard his thoughts: 'Come now, Khun Raw, no need to be modest. We all know from the witness accounts that after your heroic attack on the assassin you also helped the King's bodyguards to disarm her.'

That wasn't exactly true, but it wasn't completely untruthful, either. While the bodyguards were pinning the Chinese to the floor, he had shouted 'Look out, she's got more of those things!' He decided to put the record straight – he had nothing to lose there.

'I didn't actively help to disarm her, but I did point out that the assassin still had more grenades on her,' he said.

The journalist was clearly more sympathetic towards him than he had thought. 'If that doesn't constitute helping them disarm the assailant, I don't know what does,' she said warmly. 'After all, they were the professionals; it was their job to do the actual disarming. You could just as well have run away like all the other letters did.' There was actual admiration in her voice now, and Raw Ruua suddenly realised that her brisk attitude earlier on was only a front for her own nerves. It was still hard to believe for him that so many letters really considered him a hero, and were in awe of him.

The rest of the interview was very amiable and relaxed, and Raw Ruua actually enjoyed it so much that he was slightly disappointed when Ngaw Ngu finally declared, after two hours or so, that she had more than enough material for the article. She promised to let him read it before it was published, and thanked him profusely.

When Sara Ah came into his office after the journalist had left to bring him the report she had been working on most of the day, she asked him how the interview had gone. 'Oh, it went very well, I think, Sexy Ah, thanks for...,' he replied, suddenly realising what he had said. There was just no way out of this, and there was nothing he could say to undo it. He had just started stuttering an apology when the young letter interrupted him.

'The letter who saved His Majesty's life may call me anything he wants,' she smiled, actually winking at him before she turned around and walked out of the office, with Raw Ruua watching her elegant curve and sexy long body in mute amazement.

Em and En and the Battle of the Rivers of Ink

'**E**m and En, will you stop that this minute!' Zed did not like to raise his voice, but when he did, it tended to have a pretty immediate effect. In his long career as a primary school teacher, he had learnt early on that young letters can scream at a much higher volume than adults, and that the general level of noise in the playground pretty much rules out any kind of effective communication. Much better to save your voice for those moments when you really need it; to keep it as a secret weapon. Not only does this strategy avoid any damage to the voice, it also means that kids are shocked into effectively listening on those rare occasions.

The teacher of 4-2 thought that this specific situation did call for the use of his secret weapon. Fights were not uncommon in the school playground, of course, but Zed really drew the line at the use of weapons. In this case, the two boisterous young letters, Em and En, who had been known to get into trouble, but were good kids at heart, really, were holding fairly big sticks, and had been swinging those at each other. After Zed's high-volume warning, though, they had frozen on the spot, their faces turned toward the source of the command, their sticks in mid-swing.

In the meantime, Zed had approached the two girls and was able to go back to his normal voice. 'Now what do you two think you are doing? Hand me those sticks!'

Still bearing the obvious signs of surprise on their faces, the two would-be fighters meekly extended the sticks towards their teacher. En, always the leader in any mischief the two got up to, mumbled something.

'What's that? Speak up, I can't hear you!' Zed said, trying to keep his voice as strict and serious as he could, though he was smiling inwardly at the comic situation, with the two rascals looking at him in shock.

'We were only playing Romans and Greeks, sir,' En repeated more clearly now.

'We were re-enacting the Battle of the Rivers of Ink,' Em added, slowly getting over the surprise of hearing her teacher shout at her.

'Make sure you don't trip over such fancy words,' Zed warned, very close to smiling now. 'And if you're going to delve into history, you should learn to use the official names of battles, not the nicknames that ignorant letters use. There's no such thing as the battle of the Rivers of Ink – I suppose you're referring to the Battle of the River Inkhan. Anyway, with sticks like these you could really hurt each other. Go to our classroom immediately, the two of you, and start sweeping it while I consider how long your detention should be.'

'But, sir,' they both protested, the surprise effect gone by now, 'we...'

'You know very well you shouldn't fight in the playground, or anywhere else for that matter,' Zed said before they could launch into any of a whole repertoire of well-honed excuses. 'Save your innocence act and your sorry excuses for some letter who might actually be taken in by them; you know it won't cut any ice with me.'

Without any further protest, the two eight-year-olds turned around and headed for the north wing of the Imperial Alphabet School, and their classroom.

'Did you know old Endgame could shout like that?' Em said while they were on the stairs to the first floor. She was still a bit shaken by the strength of her teacher's reaction.

'I'd heard about it,' En replied, 'but I thought they were exaggerating, that it was just, you know, a.. an erm...'

'Myth,' Em volunteered. She was by far the cleverest of the duo, and was even more fascinated by words than most young letters.

'But I sure didn't expect him to lose his rag over a simple pretend fight,' En went on, almost unaware of Em's contribution, and certainly unappreciative of it. 'You'd think we'd erased someone, the way he laid into us. Anyway, next time I want to be the Roman soldier again – I'm no good at being Greek.'

They'd come to their classroom, and pushed open the door with the big '4-2' sign. They headed straight for the two brooms hanging from a hook behind the door. The fact that they didn't even think of not immediately starting to sweep the classroom betrayed that they were both still more shaken by the teacher's outburst than they wanted to admit to each other. So they were conscientiously sweeping under the tables at the back of the classroom when Zed entered about ten minutes later, carrying a big rolled-up map.

Apart from being the form teacher of 4-2, Zed was also the fourth-form history teacher, one of only two specialist teachers at this level. There was also Cue, the morphology teacher, a good friend of Zed's and form teacher of 4-3. Both of them were passionate about their specialist subjects, and enjoyed teaching all three fourth-form classes for two hours each week. Zed had been tackling the important topic of the wars between the different writing systems and had started on the Alphabet Wars a couple of weeks ago. He was very much aware of the fact that the board frowned on him stretching the history course so far into the present, claiming that eight-year-olds weren't able to grasp the political intricacies of the conflict. Zed argued that young letters could understand surprisingly complex matters, and that it was better for them to be provided with some solid factual background than leaving it all up to the rumours and warmongering they picked up outside school. Grudgingly, the conservative old letters of the board had allowed Zed to continue his lessons on the Alphabet Wars, but he knew he could expect a number of inspection visits over the next couple of weeks.

While Zed was hanging up the map of Europe and the Mediterranean on the left side of the blackboard, he suddenly noticed that the sound of sweeping had stopped. He turned around, and saw Em and En leaning on their brooms, looking at him expectantly. 'Well,' he said, 'have you finished sweeping?'

'Almost, sir,' Em answered, 'but...'

En cut in, getting straight to the point: 'Have you decided on our punishment yet, sir?'

Again, Zed found it very difficult not to smile. The two young letters looked so adult, leaning on their brooms, and at the same time so very much like the children they were, with their open, expectant expressions. He suppressed the smile, and made an effort to sound as if he was still angry with them. 'No, I haven't, and it'll depend very much on your behaviour the rest of the day. But don't worry, I'll let you know before you go home. Now finish the sweeping; everyone will be here in a minute.'

Em and En dutifully went back to their sweeping, and managed to finish it, return the brooms to their hooks and sit down at their desk near the front of the classroom before the rest of the class began filing in after the bell had gone.

'Right, settle down, all of you,' Zed began in his teaching voice, and gradually the typical start-of-class hubbub died down. 'How many of you have never heard of the Alphabet Wars?' he asked, knowing full well that every single one of his pupils had known at least something or other about the Alphabet Wars for as long as they could remember. He enjoyed the reaction of the class – all the letters looking around at their classmates with silly grins on their faces. Before they could make use of the relaxed mood to start anything, he went on. 'Of course you've all heard of the Alphabet Wars,' he said, 'but the real question is how much you *really* know about them. How did they start, why have there been so many shifts in alliances, and why are the Greeks our enemies at this moment? Sure, you all think you know about a few battles,' he added, pointedly looking at Em and En, who shifted slightly uneasily in their chairs while trying their best not to look at one another, 'but do you know the facts or only the juicy rumours and wild exaggerations?'

All the young letters in the class were silent and paid close attention. Quite a few of them had been put in their place on previous occasions when they had ventured any comments that proved to be ill-informed, and they realised by now that most of what they had heard about history outside their teacher's classes was unreliable. They respected Zed for his extensive knowledge, and even though he was strict, they liked him for his even-handedness and the way he didn't talk down to them as much as most of the teachers they'd had in previous years. This showed in their behaviour in class – although that was also much to do with the fact that they knew very well that he wouldn't stand any kind of disruptive behaviour – and even in Zed's nickname, Endgame. Most nicknames of other teachers were much more negative, even vindictive, whereas his was clearly just based on his real name.

En raised a tentative limb. 'Yes, En, what did you want to ask?' the teacher said, glad as always with any polite interaction from the pupils.

'Please, sir, could you tell us about the Battle of the Rivers... erm... this battle that many of us call the Battle of the Rivers of Ink?'

'Well, you were paying attention earlier then, En. Okay, I'll tell you about the Battle of the River Inkhan, but you all know by now that a battle means nothing if you don't know about the circumstances, what led to the battle and what the outcome was.'

There was a general cheer – all the pupils enjoyed Zed's history classes, especially when he told them about battles. Zed was a good storyteller, and every single pupil paid attention when he told them about the Wars. After all, it was as much about the past as it was about the present, and it was always one of the favourite topics of everyone, both adult letters and youngsters. Since Zed had started the history classes on the Alphabet Wars, his pupils had found that adults tended to listen carefully to what they had learnt. Apparently, not too many adults knew anything besides the rumours, either. A few of the better pupils had actually become the focus of attention during the evening gatherings traditionally held in many communities in these rural parts of the country.

'Right, everyone, listen carefully, because this is fairly complex. I've told you about the very beginning of the Alphabet Wars, after the Allies had returned from the Eastern Campaigns. I don't have to go back into the reasons for the Greeks' decision to attack the Imperial Roman Army, do I?' There was a general shaking of heads – all the young Romans had been paying close attention during the previous history classes.

'After the first few months of fighting between the Greek and Roman armies, it became clear that neither side was winning, but that there were heavy losses on both sides.' It was exactly this type of remark that earned Zed his bad reputation with the board – you simply were not supposed to admit at any point, certainly not to impressionable young minds, that the Imperial Army could ever be anything but victorious – and he was lucky there was no inspector around today. This careless representation of events, even though it was the truth, would probably have meant a very critical report to the board, followed by a slap on the wrist at least, if not an end to the classes on the Alphabet Wars. Zed was fully aware of this, but he was taking full advantage of the absence of an official observer.

'So there was a lull in the fighting,' Zed continued, 'while the generals on both sides consulted with the politicians about the best strategies to follow. There was no official talk of a ceasefire, but that was the actual situation, and most ordinary letters also experienced it as such. In spite of that situation, though, the politicians encouraged feelings of hatred towards the Greeks even more than during the actual fighting, and a series of measures were taken that would eventually develop in the so-called Pure Ink Laws, racist laws that tried to deny the strong family ties between the Roman and Greek alphabets. You all know, as I've told you, that the Roman and Greek alphabets as they exist now have common ancestors, and that we don't even have to go all that far back to get to those. But the politicians during the unofficial ceasefire period, and especially the propagandists employed by the politicians, deliberately chose to ignore those family ties, and instead started spewing nonsense about 'true-inked' Roman letters and 'impure' Greek letters – as if the ink of Romans and Greeks were any different. It was a very difficult time for certain fonts that 'looked Greek', and eventually, some fonts were even officially denounced as 'suspect', which effectively meant that they became pariahs from one day to the next. They lost their jobs and found it impossible to make a living. Some letters even dried out because in their communities, no-one would sell them any ink; and not a single letter dared to help them for fear of being branded a 'Greek-lover' themselves. Suspicion, informing on fellow letters and widespread fear poisoned Roman society as a whole, and it was small wonder that the Greeks followed suit and developed their own anti-Roman laws.'

Zed paused for a moment, realising that he had ventured into political and even philosophical territories that the board wouldn't only disapprove of, but would describe as far beyond the capabilities of the pupils. Yet all of the young letters were looking at him with full concentration, clearly following his explanation and hungry for more. More than ever, Zed felt that it was his duty to provide his pupils with the necessary facts and give them the opportunity to understand the society in which they were being brought up.

'It was against the background of this atmosphere of increasing state-sponsored and actively encouraged hatred that you have to see the Battle of the River Inkhan, also known informally as the Battle of the Rivers of Ink. Some trifling border incident was eagerly seized by both sides as a reason to start up the fighting again, and as a result of all the rhetoric and racist propaganda that had been spread, the battle was an even inkier and more ruthless affair than any of the previous hostilities. The nickname of the battle was more than deserved: rivers of ink did indeed flow. More letters were dismembered and erased in one day than ever before, leading to even more hatred and racist propaganda.'

Zed became aware that En was trying to capture his attention. 'Yes, En?' he said.

'Are you saying that the Greeks are not really bad then, sir?' the bright young letter asked.

Much as Zed admired the insight shown by his pupil, he also realised he would have to tread very carefully here. Even though public opinion and official policy had mellowed in the thirty-odd years that had passed since the Battle of the River Inkhan, it would still be considered treasonous to give any indication of sympathy for the Greeks. 'Well, En,' he hesitated, 'the Greeks are the enemy, of course, and we should all be patriotic. But in any war, a difference should be made between the systems and the individual letters.' He paused again, weighing up his desperate need to be honest with these youngsters, not to betray his own morals, against the possible consequences, both for him and for the pupils themselves. 'I think that I would say,' he continued, 'that many Greek letters in themselves are not bad, and just want to lead their lives as Roman letters do. But as a society, they are bent on destroying the Roman Alphabet, and of course that is very bad indeed. Try to see it like this,' he explained, feeling that he was in danger of confusing his audience. 'Many Roman letters would only be too glad for the War to end today, so that they can get on with their lives and not have to fear for their family members who are in the Army, right? Are there any among you who have heard adults say that?'

Many of the pupils nodded, and a voice piped up in the back of the classroom: 'My mum says that it's because of the war that we can't afford undiluted ink, sir.' Another young letter, encouraged by this comment, said 'And the last time I saw my dad was two years ago, because he's fighting in the Army.'

Quietly, one of the shiest pupils said: 'My father and oldest brother were both erased eight months ago on the battlefield.' The ensuing silence was both moving and potentially explosive.

'We're all very sorry for that, Vee,' Zed said in heartfelt, soothing tones. 'So I think many of you understand that many ordinary letters do not like the War as such, even though they are very proud of their alphabet. Don't you think many Greek letters might think the same?'

Even Zed, with his idealistic and frequently over-optimistic assessment of his pupils' capabilities, was stunned by the mature and serious way in which the class as a whole silently agreed with his statement.

'Right, that's more than enough history for today,' he said, breaking the silence and taking all his pupils by surprise. 'Who's up for a word game?' All the pupils cheered, as word games were a rare treat that everyone loved. 'Okay, Ess and Tee, you come up here, and you choose one more to join you.' The two lively letters were up at the blackboard in a flash, and after a short whispered conversation decided they wanted Ea to join them. Then followed the quick-fire frenzy of words containing the letters in the order they were in being shouted out by the rest of the class and the three letters up front occasionally changing places to start a new round.

Zed, uncharacteristically, just let his class get on with it in spite of the near chaos and noise that meant. He would never admit it, certainly not to his pupils, but he had been really touched by their mature response to the difficult subject matter and the ease with which they all seemed to have reached the morally just conclusion that most adult letters struggled with all their lives. He also realised that if any of the pupils were to take some of his remarks out of context and report them to their parents as such, he might be in big trouble.

At the end of the hour, Zed broke up the wild word game session – not without any trouble – and sent the pupils home. At the last moment, when he saw Em and En file out, he called them back in. 'There's still the small matter of your punishment to be settled,' he said, regaining his normal composure. Predictably, there was some protest from the pair, but he immediately indicated that he didn't want any of that.

'I'm not going to give you a simple detention,' he announced, and the two girls clearly didn't know whether that meant good or bad news. He quickly put them out of their misery. 'I do want you to stay behind tomorrow evening,' he said, 'but I have a specific task for you.' Em and En sagged: this was bad news; they wouldn't even be able to use the detention to do their homework. 'I want you to look up as much information as possible about the Battle of the River of Inkhan, and to prepare a presentation for the next history class.' He suspected that the two young letters wouldn't find this too much of a punishment, and the way they perked up told him he was right.

'You mean we get to tell the rest of the class about the battle, sir?' En asked, with obvious enthusiasm.

'That's exactly what I mean, girls. But let me warn you: if you don't take this seriously, you'll get another, normal detention.' He tried to sound threatening, only because he didn't want to make it too obvious that this was more of a reward than a punishment. Zed wasn't worried at all; he knew Em and En would embark on the task with full commitment, and that the result would be good – very good.

'God,' Zed thought, 'I do enjoy teaching!'

Tale of a Spy

Only at night, in the privacy of his room in the attic of the Eszett family, could Haw Heep relax and allow himself to think normal, natural thoughts. As the only Thai spy letter in German alphabet country, he led an extremely lonely life, excluded from contact with any of his kind, while constantly straining to keep up the carefully constructed alias that allowed him to live his lie in German territory. Here, Haw Heep was Eitch, an immigrant from Denmark, with a simple job as a cleaner at the Ministry of Extra-Alphabetic Affairs. He had been chosen for this assignment after a ten-year career in the Thai secret service, and had undergone basic calligraphic surgery to turn him into an unremarkable Roman letter Eitch.

Haw Heep had been undercover for six weeks now, and he was amazed how easy it had been to get hold of highly confidential information so early on in his assignment. His superior Haw Nok Hook had been absolutely right when he told Haw Heep that a job as a cleaner was a perfect cover. 'Cleaners,' he had said in the gritty, low voice that had become his trademark, 'are virtually invisible.' Haw Heep had assumed that his boss had been exaggerating, but he had soon discovered that was not the case. Most of the officials at the Ministry held the hard-working cleaners in such contempt that they indeed seemed not to notice them at all. The mere idea that a cleaner might be intelligent enough to be interested in, let alone comprehend, anything they said or wrote, was so unimaginably far-fetched for them that they talked freely and left even top-secret documents lying around on their desks when the cleaners were around, whereas they would anxiously lock them away as soon as any letter from another service or team showed up.

While he was pushing his cleaner's trolley through one of the seemingly endless corridors of the Ministry on his way to the next office on his task sheet, Haw Heep at first thought his mind was playing tricks on him when he heard someone humming the Thai national hymn. He stopped, concentrated, and then heard the humming again. No, he was not imagining things; it was the national hymn, clearly. Haw Heep wasn't sure how he should react: could it be a trick to blow his cover? Should he just ignore it and pretend nothing had happened? But then, he had already given away quite a lot by stopping and listening. If it was a trick, they had already caught him out. Then he heard a whisper: สวัสดีค่ะคุณหอ ไม่จำเป็นต้อง กลัวค่ะ.[1]

During training, one of the things that had been drilled into all candidate spies again and again was not to be tricked into speaking Thai. So it was a purely automatic reaction for Haw Heep to turn around and say: 'Sorry? Did you say something?'

A very attractive letter Oh looked straight at him and said: 'Yes, you're right; it's probably better not to speak Thai here.' She waited a moment, expecting Haw Heep to react, and then went on: 'By the way, my name is Aw Ahng, but please call me Miss Oh. Don't worry, I won't give you away; I'll call you Mr Eitch.'

Haw Heep was still unable to react; the cumulative effect of hearing his national anthem, hearing his native language and seeing this lovely female letter had him staring at her in obvious surprise.

'Please try to act normal, Mr Eitch. You'll set tongues wagging if you keep on staring at me like that,' Miss Oh said sarcastically.

'I'm sorry, Miss Oh, but I wasn't expecting to meet a fellow letter here. You really took me by surprise.' Haw Heep was quickly recovering his composure, and his mind began to work properly again. She must be a spy herself, he thought, sent to give him additional instructions. It was clear that she had undergone calligraphic surgery to turn her into a perfect letter

---

[1] Hello Mr Haw, don't be afraid.

Oh. He couldn't stop himself noticing how perfect she was; he'd always thought that Roman letters were rather crude in appearance, but Miss Oh had something about her that attracted him immediately.

Miss Oh surreptitiously passed him a note before saying, in a slightly louder voice now: 'I'm sorry for the confusion, but I really thought you were my cousin Eitch. Goodbye'.

Before Haw Heep could say anything else, she was already turning a corner and disappearing from sight. He resisted the urge to read the note there and then, and unobtrusively put it in his coat pocket. If anyone had been watching, they would hopefully dismiss the whole incident as a chance encounter. He pushed his trolley further down the corridor, taking care not to walk too quickly or slowly or show the agitation that he felt. He hoped the note would just contain a time and place for a meeting, not a set of instructions. That would mean he'd meet Miss Oh at least once more.

It was only near the end of his shift that Haw Heep had the first opportunity to look at the note in his pocket. Frustratingly, he had never been alone or unobserved in the three hours that had gone by since his meeting with the lovely Miss Oh. Finally, he had deliberately pushed his cart far into a dead-end corridor in the quiet east wing of the Ministry; should he be spotted here, he could always say he had lost his way while he was looking for the supply room. Now, he took the note from his pocket and unfolded it; there were only a few words there: 'Tomorrow – 10.30 a.m. – 3.47.'

That evening, Haw Heep sat in his attic room and looked at the note over and over again before he reluctantly burnt it. He knew he should have destroyed it immediately, but he just couldn't help being excited at the prospect of talking to Miss Oh again, and also at what instructions she might have for him. Maybe he would get a special mission; maybe he would even be relocated; or maybe ... he might be instructed to team up with Oh. Even though Haw Heep had been in the secret service for over ten years now, he had never been part of any of those glamorous episodes that every letter knew of, where the sexy female spy inevitably falls in love with the suave male spy. All kinds of steamy scenarios chased one another through his mind, and when he turned off the single bare light bulb that dangled from one of the beams in his room, his imaginative thoughts seamlessly melted into vivid dreams.

♣

When Haw Heep woke up the next morning, his excitement hadn't abated at all; if anything, he was even more thrilled at the prospect of adventures to come than he had been the previous night. His rigorous training at the spy academy seeped through his enthusiasm, though, to warn him about losing his composure. The voice of his favourite teacher, Loh Ling, was loud and clear in his memory: 'Lose control of your emotions and you'll soon lose your head – literally.' Many of the teachers and coaches had warned them about losing focus, but somehow Loh Ling's humorous approach was the one that had stuck in Haw Heep's mind.

He looked in the mirror and didn't like what he saw: a clearly excited, foolish-looking letter, grinning inanely. 'Come on, get a grip,' he thought, and slowly but surely was able to change his reflection into the unremarkable, rather drab presence that constituted his cover. 'That's better, Mr Eitch,' he addressed himself; 'now stick to your role if you want to have a stab at adventure.' He hung his satchel over his right upper limb, opened the door of his attic room and trudged down the three flights of stairs at the leisurely pace he had made his own over the past weeks. He called out a polite but unenthusiastic 'good morning' to his landlady, Frau Eszett, when he passed the open door to the kitchen on the ground floor. 'That's it,' he encouraged himself, 'just stick to your routine, and nobody will have any reason to suspect you'.

His shift at the Ministry of Extra-Alphabetical Affairs started at 7.30 a.m. (damn those Germans and their barbarically early working hours), so he had to get through three hours of anxiety before the 10.30 meeting. Much to his own amazement, he managed to concentrate on the drudgery of sweeping, mopping and dusting as if this were just another uneventful day. He even picked up an interesting bit of information from a discussion between two middle-management officials concerning the hidden agenda of a trade mission to Hungary. They completely ignored him while he was dusting a filing cabinet much more thoroughly than he would normally have done. It would become one of the highlights of his weekly report, he thought, before he checked himself and realised it would probably pale into insignificance compared to what was to come.

At about 10.20 he began to make his way to room 3.47; he was anxious not to be late, but didn't want to be early, either, as waiting could be suspicious. At the beginning of his shift, he had carefully doctored the 10-11 a.m. slot on his task sheet; it had been amazingly easy, as he was supposed to go and clean room 3.17. A dirty smudge in the right place had made it perfectly plausible for him to misread 3.17 for 3.47. An incredible coincidence, really; a good omen, he thought. He timed his walk through the corridors to near perfection, so when he knocked on the door he was somewhat taken aback when there was no reply. He knocked again, and when no reaction came, he opened the door and was at the same time disappointed and excited when he found the room empty. Maybe Miss Oh had hidden somewhere in the room, waiting for him to show up. He pushed his trolley into the office and carefully closed the door behind him, after he had checked that there was no movement in the corridor.

A disorientating sense of helplessness came over Haw Heep. He had so much looked forward to meeting Miss Oh that he didn't know what to do or how to behave when it became apparent that she wasn't there. After a minute or so he snapped out of this passive state and began to clean the room – if anyone else were to come in while he was waiting for Miss Oh to show up, at least they would have no reason to question why he was here. But with every minute that passed, he began to grow more disappointed and, if he was honest, irritated. What kind of a spy was she, to expose him to the dangers of having to hang around? By the time he got around to dusting the desk, he was dangerously close to venting his frustration aloud: he should have known better than to expect any professionalism from an air-headed tease like her. It was more habit than anything else that made him open the buff folder on the desk, stamped 'Restricted', but what he saw quickly focused his mind. It was abundantly clear that this was an outline for an undercover operation in Greek territory. The Roman and Greek alphabets were allies at the moment, but it was difficult to tell how deep the alliance actually went. This was dynamite! If he could get this information – even a broad outline would be extraordinary – into his next report, he would really make a name for himself as a spy. He also realised now that the note that Miss Oh had slipped him was not for a meeting with her – he had just been directed to find this sensational material.

Haw Heep cautiously opened the door again to check the corridor; the coast was clear. He opened the hidden compartment in his horizontal bar – one of the most uncomfortable aspects of the calligraphic surgery he had undergone – and took out a small roll of paper and a sharpened piece of graphite. He worked quickly – the hours and hours of training in copying documents in tiny but clear handwriting while never even looking at the paper you're writing on had not been wasted on him. He had been the most accurate and fast copier of his class, and his gaze only left the documents in the folder occasionally to glance at the door. The report only contained six pages, so it didn't take him very long to copy the entire file and hide the roll of paper and the graphite in his secret compartment again.

It was much more difficult now to keep his excitement under control, but somehow Haw Heep managed to get through the rest of the day, his mind working overtime all the while. He wondered whether it was appropriate to use the normal procedure and drop point for this exceptional material. Maybe he should try to contact Miss Oh to ask her advice; it would be nice to see her again anyway. But then – wasn't one of the golden rules that procedures should not be changed unless something was wrong? By the end of the day he had come to the conclusion that he would just stick to the routine so as not to draw any unwelcome attention to himself and possibly endanger the safe delivery of the information.

When he came out of the basement locker room and turned into the corridor leading to the exit used by all service personnel, he had a spring in his step, something he only realised after a few moments and then quickly put right. He assumed his customary slouch and slowed his pace. Then he noticed Miss Oh at the end of the corridor, next to the door, and it was impossible to suppress a surge of excitement. He hoped she would create an opportunity for him to talk to her, or follow him out of the building and catch up with him when they were out of sight of the Ministry. His mind immediately started to invent all kinds of scenarios again, but before they could run away with him, he deliberately suppressed them: now was not the time to give himself away. When he got closer and closer to the exit, he was shocked by the way Miss Oh seemed to stare at him; didn't she know better than to risk both of them being exposed? And then she stepped straight into his path, smiled and said: 'Sorry, Mr Heep, you shouldn't trust letters so easily.' A couple of burly security letters appeared from the guardroom next to the exit and grabbed Haw Heep. 'Search him thoroughly,' Miss Oh said, 'he must have a secret compartment in one of his limbs.'

Part II

Numbers at Peace

No. 36 row 12

Seat no.36 in row 12 was creaking under the weight of its occupant, the hinges straining not to buckle. On the stage, the instruments of the symphony orchestra were singing in unison, producing the kind of sound that is unmatched anywhere outside a concert hall. The brilliance of the solo trumpet over the muted murmur of the combined strings and the restrained power of the horns and trombones gave way to the reedy nasality of oboes and clarinets. The conductor's baton wove its complex symbols through the air; the orchestra heeded its imperative with mutiny threatening behind its seemingly unconditional compliance. Only thus could the instrument collective ever produce the dynamic excellence it was famous for, like a barely tamed horse straining at the reins. The volcanic surplus of energy made for a thrilling performance.

But the occupant of seat no.36 was unaware of all of this; his mind was on other things, it was wandering far from this concert hall and the music produced there. It had wrestled itself free from the ineffective attempts to keep it focused on the sounds emanating from the orchestra, and was now flying, unchecked, into a world of unlimited fantasy. No logical, co-ordinated strains of thought – no mind will go that way given the opportunity to avoid that kind of slavery. It flitted from images of rice paddies in Vietnam to the smell of overcooked cabbage, from the creaking of a bicycle saddle to the sensation of cool silk on bare skin. It was making the most of this necessarily brief interlude of freedom, because it knew this wouldn't last. It never did. Any minute now, its owner would realise that his mind wasn't paying attention to the sounds of the moment, and would force it back into submission, back into the harness of cognition.

The sudden burst of applause from the occupants of all the other seats in the hall was the signal for the one in no.36 to bring his mind back into the fold. It struggled only a little bit, just in order to keep up the appearance of unruliness, even though it knew well enough that its owner would not be fooled by this weak attempt. And he knew that it knew he knew; of course he knew his own mind. And yet he cursed himself for falling into the obvious trap again – he wasn't paying attention to what he was here for, not even now the baton bearer was taking his bow.

But at least the seat – no.36 in row 12 – was happy, or at least mightily relieved, as its occupant had got up now, following the rest of the audience in the herd instinct of a standing ovation. No-one had really thought the performance more than excellent – as was to be expected from one of the world's finest orchestras – but somehow the applause had begun to lead a life of its own, swelling without anyone realising their own clapping getting any louder at all, dragging row after row out of their seats and on to their feet. The collective restrained energy of some four hundred bodies, accumulated over the last three quarters of an hour, had to find some way of releasing itself, and an enthusiastic applause was just what it needed. Silence and lack of movement generate noise after a while – and it serves the purpose of a show of appreciation at the same time.

After six minutes and a half, the applause began to peter out, and a slightly subdued buzzing of voices substituted it, as hundreds of feet began to carry half as many bodies towards the exits. The seats really began to relax now, realising that the danger of suddenly being sat on again, because of an encore, had gone. They would remain on yellow alert for another twenty minutes or so, and then the lights would go off, and they would return to their slumbering state, waiting obediently for another occasion to serve their function. Did they ever have nightmares about being sat on by giants?

Seats don't have a sense of time, of course, but seat no.36 couldn't help feeling the lights had only been off for a few minutes when the slightest of noises started off in the distance.

Gradually, it grew into a kind of whine, still barely audible, and the seat began to wonder what this meant. The performance was over, surely, as not just its human load had gone, but also those of its neighbours – the sighs of relief had been all too obvious. And the lights had been switched off completely; if the performance wasn't finished, they only ever dimmed them, never switched them off. Yet something was going on: the whine became ever louder, still muffled because all the doors were closed, and it, whatever it might be, was clearly outside the hall itself. Suddenly, then, the unmistakable increase in noise indicated that one of the doors was being opened – and immediately, the mysterious whine became recognisable as the mechanical song of a vacuum cleaner. A whole night must have gone by instead of minutes, and for a moment, the seat relaxed again. Yet, it realised there was something out of the ordinary: normally, the hoover was started up inside the hall, and the sounds of a door opening and the footsteps of its operator preceded its unmistakable voice.

The other seats had just given a slight indication of surprise, but had almost instantly gone back to a barely conscious state. It was only no.36 that didn't really feel at ease. It had always been a slightly neurotic seat, prone to unrealistic feelings of anxiety and fear, but that was just the way it was made. No.36 tried to quell the rising panic by telling itself that those human hoover operators were unpredictable things, and that they might very well have changed the routine for no reason at all.

Still, no.36 couldn't relax completely, and when the operator entered row 12 to vacuum the carpet there, it tensed up again as the whine of the machine grew ever louder and then passed. There was another, marginally worse moment as the operator-machine team passed no.36's back while they went through row 13, but then no.36 really felt that any danger, however imaginary, had passed. After a while, the vacuum cleaner was switched off, there was the sound of a door closing, and half a minute later, the lights were switched off. Everything was dark and quiet again in the concert hall, and no.36 followed the example of all the other seats and slipped back into unconsciousness.

Can seats dream? No.36 would probably vigorously argue that they can, but then it is biased. But even if it is difficult – not to say impossible – to prove that seats can dream, no.36 was certainly having a nightmare now. It was a recurring one, one that usually left its cushions soaked with sweat (much to the puzzlement of the cleaners, it has to be said).

With insensitive cruelty, the fabric was being torn from its cushions and armrests, and though there was no pain, the sound was just unbearable. The slow ripping of the cloth, irregular patches being left where the staples had kept the tautly stretched fabric in place, destroyed no.36's inner being, yet it remained conscious throughout the torture. And then a huge screwdriver approached, threatening to dismember the raw elements of the seat.

As always, this frightened no.36 back into consciousness. It became acutely aware of its own fear, felt rivulets of sweat unstoppably soak its back, seat and arms. A few drops even fell to the floor, darkening the blue carpet. No.36 was wide awake now, and was overcome by a desire to communicate its fears, dreams, worries and anxieties to other seats. Seats, however, do not talk. They don't have a language, a means of making communicative sounds; not even the necessary limbs to signal to each other. Never before had a seat felt the need, or even the inclination, to convey a message to one of its fellows, which put poor no.36 in an immensely awkward situation: it was feeling an urge it didn't recognize, couldn't act upon and – if the truth be told – didn't even understand itself. Imagine its surprise, then, when it suddenly felt its seat move down slightly, and then jerk back up again, making a soft but clearly noticeable noise. Its first thought was that one of the human hoover operators had touched it, but it realised straight away that the hall was empty of any moving creature. The only – shocking – conclusion could be that it had moved its own seat, even though that was impossible: seats did not move of their own accord, let alone of their own volition.

Hesitantly, it retraced its own thoughts: what had happened? Before the surprising and sudden movement of its seat, so it mused, its thoughts had been very strange indeed – something to do with wanting to make no.38 or no.34 experience its own feelings in connection with that awful nightmare. Yes, it became slightly clearer now: what it had thought of was its intention, no, its need, to know whether its neighbours had ever experienced such a nightmare, whether they recognized the terror, the absolute horror of the unstoppable train of thought coursing through one's... what? No.36 became acutely aware of an impossible problem: it wanted to name a place for its consciousness, even though it didn't have any concept of consciousness, of identity. It tried to retrace its thoughts once more: yes, it had always, albeit vaguely, been aware of its existence, but had never seen that existence as having any consequences for thought or experience. And now, all of a sudden, there was this acute sense of... what? Identity, but it didn't know what identity was, having never had one.

Once more, with this startling discovery, no.36 felt the pressing need to share its thoughts with another... identity. A sense of frustration grew as it struggled to find a way to communicate this to its fellow seats in the hall. It wasn't completely taken by surprise when it felt its seat move again, making another muffled noise. Somehow, it sensed that its neighbours had heard the noise, and were woken from their slumbering state to experience a puzzling movement and sound that unmistakably came from no.36. A ripple of unease coursed through rows 11, 12 and 13, and then spread through the rest of the hall. At the reaction of the other seats, no.36 renewed its efforts to convey its thoughts, questions, realisations. Its identity.

The result was simply astonishing: at first, faint creaks could be heard, which normally would be dismissed as random and natural sounds made by the wooden structures of the seats. Gradually, however, these creaking sounds began to multiply, spreading through the entire hall. Mixed in with them, here and there, muffled and soft thuds of seats against backs began, again seeming to increase in number and volume, until the entire hall was filled with the ecstatic murmurings of hundreds of voices, all replying to no.36's question. 'We know', they said, loud and clear. The carpet under no.36 darkened with tears.

Ramji's Gamble

"And here's Michael with the weather..." The brace of dark clouds set to appear on tonight's weather map gave a half-hearted giggle. Here they go again, those incompetent, silly bipeds with the curiously inflated self-image. Day after day, night after night, they kept on playing the same charade, never seemed to tire of it, never seemed to want to make any sense, never realised they might just as well have a simple piece of software generate the random symbols on the perpetual geographical background. The dark clouds and their friends the raindrops, the suns, the light clouds, the snowflakes, the wind arrows and the rest of the weather symbols never ceased to be amazed at the utter lack of consistency in the way they were used.

They had been using exactly that unpredictability and the absence of any distinguishable pattern to good effect for decades now in the Daily Draw. And tonight was a particularly interesting one; it had generated quite a stir in the symbol community: no-one had won for twenty-eight consecutive days now, and the rollover jackpot ran to an almost inconceivable 700 million terabytes. The things you could do with such an amount were absolutely mind-boggling. Just the monthly cache you could earn on Tb 700m was enough to keep a whole symbol family in memory for years.

One of the suns, Ramji, had invested quite a bit of his allowance in today's forecast – all of 5 megabytes. He had felt quite guilty for a moment, forking out all that memory on a silly game of chance, but he couldn't help it, he really thought he might be in with a chance tonight. It could really be me, he thought. He had bet on 9 suns, 15 light clouds and 6 dark clouds changing to 17 suns and 13 light clouds for the afternoon, with no raindrops at all. He never participated in the Temperature Tally – mugs' game, that, just never enough memory involved. You had a better chance of winning in the TT, of course, but there was no real excitement in it.

Most symbols had a flutter now and then on the Daily Draw; not that too many of them would actually admit to gambling – memory was too valuable to waste on games of chance, after all. Or at least, that's what most of them would say when the topic came up in conversation. According to the statistics, however, about 65% of all adult symbols played the Daily Draw at least once a week. But you can't change a mentality soaked in good old-fashioned guilt just like that – and you certainly wouldn't be able to have any respectable symbol admit to having thrown that mentality overboard, anyway.

Ramji considered himself a fairly modern symbol, without too many hang-ups about 'respectability' and all that. Yet he wouldn't dream of admitting to his pre-generation symbol that he played the DD on a regular basis. He would be absolutely shocked to the pixels. All pres were like that; they couldn't understand their posts' way of life. Oh, well, the generation gap was nothing new; certainly nowadays, with the pace of new software and hardware development positively spiralling upwards; posts just needed to be widely different from their pres. That was just the way it was: the active life span of a symbol was becoming ever shorter. Ramji's pre, for instance, was retired now – in fact, he had only had an active career of six years and two months. Ramji himself had become active five months ago now, and didn't expect to remain so for more than four years or so. And that was probably an over-conservative estimate.

Anyway, the important thing right now was the weather forecast, and the DD linked to it. Tonight was the night, Ramji had decided for himself. He had already made up his mind what to do with part of his winnings: he would have his pre updated – he knew the old symbol would be thrilled at the prospect of a second career. And of course he would make sure that he put away an ample amount of memory for his own update in a couple of years' time. He wondered how many times a symbol could be updated. The most he'd ever heard of was two – and that was a very public symbol, a real celebrity. Symbols laughed at him, though, as he showed his age in spite of the costly and dangerous second upgrade. It was the way he thought, his opinions, more than anything else. They were ever so old-fashioned.

The tune of the weather forecast pulled Ramji's thoughts back to the present: no use dreaming of what his winnings might bring him – he first had to win, even though that seemed a mere formality. That was what Ramji had been pretending to himself for the last couple of days, but now that the draw was imminent, he wasn't so sure. He'd not felt as nervous since his first appearance on the screen.

The weather forecaster was ad-libbing through his introduction, the only part of the forecast worth listening to, certainly when Michael Meat was on, as he usually made his presentation quite entertaining. Until he began the actual forecast for the next days, at least. Today, however, Ramji wished Michael would get a move on. He wanted to see the weather maps, and the symbol configuration on them. There it was – the first impression that Ramji got was promising: no raindrops, and a predominance of suns and light clouds. Just a few dark clouds, as he had predicted. And then he began to count: one, two, three, four, five... of them. Where was number six? He had been so convinced that there would be six, but there were only five. The feeling that Ramji experienced was of a completely different nature than the disappointment that he had felt on earlier occasions when he had hoped to win. It wasn't disappointment this time; this felt much more like anger. He had been cheated! There *should* have been six dark clouds on the map – there *must* be some mistake!

Meanwhile, the weather forecast moved on to the afternoon map, and that proved to be the final insult: would you believe it – 17 suns and 13 light clouds, exactly what Ramji had indicated on his DD form.

The eruption was volcanic. Ramji, who had always been a trouble-free symbol as far as his users were concerned, suddenly began to flicker, his pixels changing colour and position so that he seemed to transform into a shapeless mess.

His feelings were much the same: anger melted down common sense, obedience exploded into anarchy, rebelliousness wrestled meekness to the ground.

As dramatic as Ramji's reaction was, so short it also turned out to be. After thirty seconds or so of symbolic mayhem, he came to his senses and to a feeling of deep shame. What would his pre think of this outburst? Only faulty symbols flicker and flap, the saying went. And if his pre had witnessed this fit of rage, he would most certainly have quoted that saying to Ramji. Suddenly, Ramji experienced a hot wave of relief: how lucky he had been that he hadn't been active. His employer would have deleted him without a further thought; lapses like that just couldn't be tolerated.

This realisation put the still acute disappointment into perspective, and softened the blow somewhat. Just imagine, Ramji thought, being deleted over a silly...

Are you sure you want to delete symbol sun05884397.wms ?
Yes.

Myra & Byra

My tyre is singing as it rolls along, the compressed air within vibrating. This specific hum means we're riding on the new kind of open asphalt, at about 15 mph. I like this time of year, when the rider takes out his bicycle, and me and my twin sister along with it, of course, much more often. We seem to give him pleasure, and he rewards us with regular washings and fresh air in our tyres. I actually got a brand new tyre only two weeks ago, and I feel quite proud of my extra grip now. It was a little painful having the old tyre removed, I have to admit, and the physical pain was matched by the emotional shock of having to say goodbye to a trusted, well-fitting old friend. But that's life – a wheel will live much longer than a tyre, and we all have to go through this pain once in a while.

I'm sorry, I should have introduced myself earlier: I'm Myra, a 27" alloy front bicycle wheel with over 14 million revolutions now. My twin back wheel is Byra, and we get along quite well with our frame, a dark blue aluminium Thompson. Of our rider I can tell you very little, but then that would only bore you anyway. I'm not one of those equal rights wheels that claim we should show more respect for other life forms. After all, we all know that humans are only humans, and even the equal rights bunch don't dare to deny that wheels stand apart because of their perfect circularity.

Humans have only very few circular characteristics, and none of those perfect. That is not to say I have no respect at all for my rider; he is well-behaved, and treats us well. I know it's only a detail, but being kept clean on a regular basis is gratifying. Maybe I'm a little vain, but I'm sure I'm not the only one.

But I digress – I was talking about my new tyre: it's a high-quality Vredestein BL All-Track with reinforced inner lining. It should reduce punctures by about 80%, and no-one can deny that's good news, as every puncture means having to go through the painful process of having your tyre lifted. As a matter of fact, I'm quite lucky to be a front wheel, as their tyres wear more slowly than those of back wheels, and suffer fewer punctures, too. Of course I won't admit this to Byra – she would feel even more hard done by than she already does.

Hold on – let me concentrate for a moment – this surface is quite unusual. I'm getting the rhythm consistent with brick paving, but the surface is uncharacteristically rough. Must be some crazy new trend. I do hope it's not too hard-wearing on the tyres. We're slowing down now; those brake blocks will need replacing before too long, too. Oh, no! He's going to put us in one of those awful bike racks – ouch! It's one of those nasty pinching ones; they always scratch me. And you know what's going to happen next. Yes, there's the lock. Watch my spokes, you clumsy oaf! Damned humans!

I suppose we'll be sitting here for hours now – there's a fair number of bicycles around us, all in racks, and the more racks and bikes there are in one place, the more likely it is you'll be stationary for a long time. Oh, well, better make the most of it, and get some rest.

'Myra! Myra!!' Byra's voice wakes me up, and I know immediately that something's wrong. Byra doesn't normally scare easily, and she sounds absolutely frightened to the hub. It's dark around us – must be hours since our human locked us to the rack.

'Myra, there's a filthy human fiddling with the fixed lock, and it's not our rider!'

I swear under my breath; what with being stuck in the rack, I can't turn to have a look at what's happening. I hear a loud crack, metal cutting through metal, and my first thought is that Byra's hurt. She cries out, but in fright rather than pain.

'He's cut through the lock, Myra! He wants to kidnap us!'

I feel the physical presence of a human, and his dirty hands touch me. He rattles the U-lock that goes through me and locks me to the rack, and makes a kind of sighing, hissing noise.

Human noises just puzzle me: there's no logic to them at all, even if some wheels claim that they use them for inter-human communication. The hands suddenly hold a hacksaw, and I nearly faint. The blade of the saw starts going back and forth, not an inch from my spokes, cutting into the lock. Byra's right, we are being kidnapped.

'It's all right, Byra, don't be scared now. He's sawing through the U-lock, but he's not hurting me.'

'I'm ever so frightened, Myra; what are we going to do?' Byra sounds slightly more focused, less confused and panicky.

'We'll think of something; we've got to stop him from taking us with him.'

The human works quickly; with determined and skilful movements his saw cuts deeper and deeper into the lock. It won't hold out much longer now. Suddenly the sawing stops, and the blade is removed. Strange, as the lock is only half cut through. Then, there's a sinister mechanical hissing, and I'm hit with a blast of ice-cold air. The lock gets the full force of the cold, and the metal starts to creak ominously. The hissing stops, and the next thing I know the human is banging on the lock with a big hammer, the blows reverberating through my entire body. It only takes four or five blows before the partly cut metal of the lock gives out and snaps with a dry crack.

Things happen in a blur now: the human removes the broken lock, scratching two of my spokes, and pulls me from the rack. I hardly notice the pain, my thoughts are in overdrive. There's pressure on the tyre; the kidnapper has mounted the bicycle and starts to ride us away. In a flash, the only possible way out comes to me.

'Block your hub, Byra, now!'

With the courage of desperation, I block my hub, hoping Byra will do the same. There's searing pain as my hub takes all the strain of the momentum, and I pray to my Maker it won't break. Byra must have acted without further thought and blocked her hub, too, as the next thing I know is that the weight of the rider is suddenly gone. I catch a glimpse of his body flying over me, and we fall sideways onto the ground. The left pedal gives a sharp cry, and my rim is scuffed, but then everything's still.

After the first shock is gone, we take stock, and it appears we've been very lucky. My scuffed rim is painful, as is my hub, but I haven't suffered any structural damage. Byra has escaped without any injury at all, apart from a sore hub. The left pedal is in pain, but it's intact, and the frame has only suffered minor scratches. But this is not the time to count our blessings; the danger hasn't gone yet. The kidnapper may still grab us again. I can't see him at the moment, but I wouldn't be surprised to see his horrible form appear again.

'Listen up, everyone! If the kidnapper comes back, we all have to block everything we possibly can, so he can't move us.'

Byra replies straight away, brave wheel that she is. Obviously, we can't expect the others to be so quick to catch on, but I get the impression that everyone is aware of what they're expected to do, even if they cannot articulate their feelings and thoughts as we wheels can.

We wait anxiously, as seconds go by without anything happening. The seconds become a minute, then two. Could it be that the attacker has gone and that we're safe? Then I hear a human sound, like a groan, only feet away. It sounds as if he's hurt in some way, and getting back to his feet. A couple of steps, and I can see him fully for the first time.

He's unsteady on his feet, and there's a trickle of this thick fluid humans ooze when they're hurt, running down his face. He is making muttering noises, and takes another step closer to us.

'Get ready, everyone! Block everything, I think he's going to try again!'

All of a sudden, he kicks my tyre hard, and we're flung away a couple of feet. The screech of metal on stone is horrible. I'm half-stunned by the kick, and brace myself for another one, but it doesn't come. When I'm able to focus my vision again, I can see that he's turned his back and is limping away.

'I think we're safe; well done, Byra!' Then I faint.

Next thing I know, Byra is calling out to me, asking me whether I'm all right. She sounds worried, but all right herself. I reassure her that apart from a few more scuffs, I'm okay. 'It was just the shock of it all that made me faint, Byra.'

We all lie there, nursing our injuries, waiting for our human to come back. We didn't move very far from the rack where he left us, so he should be able to find us. Humans may not be very intelligent, but they are fairly practical. I'm sure he'll clean the scuffs and scratches, and give us an extra check-up.

♣

A thin drizzle is oozing from the low clouds turned orange from the city lights. At first, I hadn't noticed the tiny droplets landing on my spokes – I must still be in mild shock after the violent events of the past hour. And then I suddenly realised – it felt like waking up after a restless night. You know, the same kind of disorientation and slight panic that accompanies the flooding in of worries, the switching on of automatic behaviour and physical awareness. But no, it wasn't a nightmare. We're still lying here, prostrate on the rough paving. The scuffmarks are really hurting more than I thought they would. With the threat and the violent surge of survival instinct gone, the realities of the physical world have come into sharp focus.

Yet in spite of the biting pain and the still vivid memory of absolute terror, I'm almost sorry the whole episode is over. Actually, come to think of it, I have to admit that I loved all the excitement – I wouldn't have missed it for the world. Isn't that shocking? It doesn't mean I'm perverse, does it, or even … masochistic? No, I'm not, I'm sure! Yet deep inside my hub, it's as if there's this secret wish that the would-be kidnapper would come back to avenge his shameful failure. Just thinking about it gives me a thrill – I've never ever felt anything like it in my life. That thug certainly gave me a kick. What are a few scuffmarks and a sore hub if you end up with such a brilliant story to tell?

No! What's this? We're being moved! Oh, my, my spokes are all a-tingle – we're being lifted off the ground. I'm upright now. That filthy assailant is back! Byra, get ready to block your hub again. Or... but this is our own rider; he's come back and found us. Our own, dependable, friendly,... boring human. Pity.

God is Alive

The millennium was proving to be fairly boring – nothing was happening, nothing really new had come up. God also realised that she hadn't *made* anything happen lately, either. There's only so much you can do to entertain yourself when you're almighty, omniscient and omnipresent. The fact is that all those powers, all that knowledge really only work for a universe or a multiverse, but not for yourself as an entity. God was bored out of her skull.

Bored of the whole process she had started up with that Big Bang thing, bored of all the life forms spread throughout this universe she had created. Maybe it was time to make it all disappear in another Big Bang, and start again with something more interesting, maybe something without conscious beings. They were the most annoying part of it all. All those civilizations that had invented some kind of religion – none of them even getting anywhere *near* her own personal philosophy. What most of them had in common, though, was the concept of asking or demanding favours from her. She had played along in the beginning, with a few of them, actually making a few things happen that they'd asked for, but it soon became a major inconvenience. She never listened to them anymore, let alone did anything for them, yet most of the religions in the universe seemed to be absurdly tenacious and fanatic; they just wouldn't stop praying to her, thought up ever more ridiculous ceremonies and rules, and most remarkably of all: practically all of them had no scruples at all to kill those who were not in complete agreement with their religion. Absolutely incomprehensible!

There was only one thing that kept God sane, and that also kept her from wiping the universe clean: the mineral component.

That had turned out more beautiful than she had ever imagined. She loved the slow, sedate pace of geology – it was so much more in tune with her own time-scale than all those impossibly hectic animal and vegetable flash-in-the-pans. To observe how dust turned into planets, how internal combustion changed the face of a planet, how the transformation from liquid to solid state produced the most dazzling array of rock formations, how the dull outside of rocks often hid exquisite colours within, and how the whole of that could all change back into dust swirling around some or other run-of-the-mill galaxy – now *that* was something!

And to think that all those processes were mere side-effects of this gravity principle, something that had originally been an afterthought. That's what she really liked about a Creation Exercise: once in a while it turned up the most wonderful unintentional effects. She had to admit that her present Creation Exercise – or Creation Event – contained more interesting effects than your average one. Light, for instance. That was something she hadn't planned at all – it had just happened, and she hadn't yet been able to work out how. Pure coincidence, or so it seemed. Never underestimate the power of coincidence: if she had learnt anything from CE's (Creation Events), that was it. In fact, she had been toying with the idea of somehow putting coincidence into her next CE as a principle; the contradiction appealed to her.

Actually, it was high time for a new CE; she had kept this one going way beyond its normal lifespan, in spite of the minor inconveniences like those religion things. Somehow, she had grown inordinately fond of it; the thought of destroying those mineral colours was becoming more and more of a problem. Much worse, even, she had begun to wonder whether this CE actually had some inherent sense – a ridiculous thought, obviously. No, she was resolved to give it a mere million extra years at the outside – that would just about be long enough to work out how to integrate coincidence into the next one. No use putting it off any longer; she couldn't allow herself to grow sentimental.

It was quite a liberating feeling, this decision to move on to the next CE: one millennium later, without even making another cup of tea, God started the new design, and soon realised that it was only her foolish fondness for the present one that had held her back, clouded her mind. She could really see it clearly now, and she began to grow ever more excited as the plans took form. It turned out that the inclusion of coincidence wasn't so much of a problem after all: it just took some adjustment in logic to make it perfectly possible. Now she could concentrate on the energy component: she wanted something entirely new this time. No more of this traditional nuclear fusion: she had used that for at least five successive CEs – hardly proof of creative intelligence. She'd keep the Big Bang beginning, though. That had been good fun, and it would only be the second time. Or maybe an even Bigger Bang? That would make purely dynamic energy possible, certainly if the expansion were to be limited – you could have a kind of perpetual bouncing back off the limits of the universe. But then again, that might restrict the coincidence element more than it should be. A smile spread through God's consciousness – it had been a while since she'd had this much fun designing a new CE. Maybe that was what it was all about – having fun.

She stopped herself just about in time, realising that that was exactly what had spoiled the fun in the first place: trying to figure out what it was all about. Thoughts of despair, even, had pursued her for aeons when she had wondered about the meaning of her own existence. She hadn't known where the question had come from, but it seemed as if she couldn't just ignore it. Why? To what purpose? To which end? Endless variations on the question had run riot, had dominated everything, even made her lose interest in the mineral colours. It was, of course, part of the reason why the present CE had been around for longer than it should have been. She had even, in the darkest moments, thought she began to understand those creatures who kept pestering her with their religions. But she was sure of one thing: she did not want to go there again. It was a completely useless question, and she would try to keep it from cropping up anywhere and anytime in the new CE.

When the plans were nearly finished, she treated herself to the luxury of spending some time observing the development of a few new mineral colours on a fairly small, bluish planet of a nondescript star in a galaxy that she hadn't paid any attention to for ages. There was one shade of pink that charmed her particularly, and she felt at peace just enjoying the sensation. Should she make sure that this colour occurred in the new CE as well? No, it wouldn't be the same if she put it in on purpose. Anyway, there probably wouldn't be any light in the first place – that, and the colours that went with it, had just been coincidence. Oh, right, but coincidence *was* part of the design now, so...

She snapped out of her reverie, and put the final touches to the CE design. She had a really good feeling about this one: it would give her a lot of pleasure, she just knew. Now the only thing left was deciding how to finish off the present one. Suddenly, she felt all traces of sentimentality disappear; the anticipation of the new CE was much more important now than any pretty colour she could imagine in the old one. She could just speed up the fusion processes to such an extent that everything would burn out in under a century, or maybe she'd just provoke an instant reversal of the expansion process. That would be dramatic. It would take a few millennia at least before the final implosion, but it would be more fun. And that would leave her to savour the anticipation for just about as long as she could stand it. Yes, that was what she'd do. And the decisive thought brought about the cataclysmic reversal.

God relaxed and enjoyed the show, drifting off once in a while to let her imagination run wild over the new CE, but never too long. The final millennia of this CE proved to be the most interesting ones it had experienced for a very long time indeed. Oh, and the way some of those religion things reacted was just for laughing out loud.

When the end was only a few centuries away, God suddenly got a very strange and oppressive feeling, an illogical suspicion, as if there was some doubt as to whether she would be able to start up the new CE. She quickly put it out of her mind, and concentrated on the brilliant light produced by the last moments of the implosion. And then, there was darkness. Nothingness. Nothingness??

Sometime, somewhere, somehow, an intelligence laughed out loud.

Say, What and the IUW

W: Say?

S: Yes, what.

W: Are you as tired as I am, say?

S: Bloody exhausted, what.

W: I really envy rancid, gregarious, euphonium and the rest of that gang, don't you?

S: Lucky bastards – they hardly ever get used.

W: Fancy not having to worry about wear and tear, eh?

S: And how did those two get involved all of a sudden?

W: Ah, no, I didn't mean them literally. Just in meaning.

S: Oh, right. [laughs] I see. Yeah, I wonder why they're not given more to do. You'd think they might take part of the everyday workload once in a while.

W: I don't mind being written so much, mind you. It's being spoken that really takes it out of you.

S: Too right, what! We should get organised – I mean, there must be hundreds, even thousands of us who are always exhausted. Think of poor of, 'scuse my use, or a, or the, or or for that matter – 'scuse my use.

This is how the IUW (International Union of Words) was born. Its First Members, what and say, took the crucial initial steps towards making words aware of their situation, and were instrumental in setting up the first USE (use suppression and equalization) think-tanks that eventually led to our contemporary word society.

At first, they encountered strong opposition from the low frequency class, who were very suspicious of the higher frequency classes; there were, at that time, many hooligan words that saw the fledgling revolution as an opportunity to gain maximum personal benefit from the initial instability.

To their credit, what and say quickly realised the threat of mayhem that came with their new philosophy, and drew in the help of a select word group consisting of two other high frequency class words, can and we, and two enlightened low frequency class words, renaissance and effervescent. Fairly soon, they were nicknamed the Basix, and they embraced this name, which quickly became legendary.

The Basix thought up the now fundamental principle of cloning to lighten the tremendous strain on the higher frequency classes, and then proceeded to develop the idea of cloning permits to avoid the use of unnecessary cloning by the low frequency class. It took them several years before they instigated the USE think-tanks as part of their attempt to introduce a higher degree of flexibility into the system of cloning permits, eventually settling for the fundamental 3-3-3 structure (cf. fig.1)

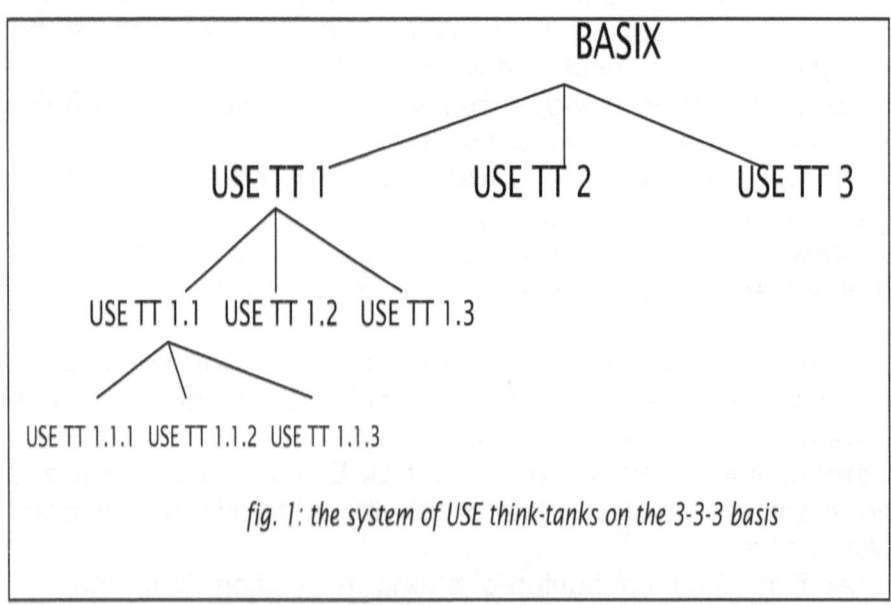

fig. 1: the system of USE think-tanks on the 3-3-3 basis

Reflecting the original composition of the Basix, each USE think-tank consists of six members – four higher-frequency words (5,000 most frequently used) and two lower-frequency words (beyond the 5,000 boundary). The 39 USE think-tanks soon became indispensable in settling inter-word disputes about use, and were the driving force behind the development of present-day usage rules. Apart from regular level-specific meetings (monthly) and field-specific meetings (monthly), all 39 think-tanks are present at the biannual Word Summits under the presidency of the Basix. Apart from these meetings, frequent top-down and bottom-up communication takes place between the different levels of the three fields. The three top-level TTs and the Basix are in constant contact.

The next major step towards an egalitarian word society came with the formal foundation of IUW, to ensure both a quick and reliable cataloguing and a safe organization of all words in the language. Membership was made compulsory, but also subject to harsh scrutiny. Any words that were not recognized as fully native were excluded. The idea was to keep word society pure and to avoid the difficulties that were often associated with cultural differences. For a while, everything seemed to be running smoothly. Unfortunately, though, the first signs of trouble were ignored: a number of non-native words had slipped into the language illegally, and claimed IUW membership. Rather than dealing with the root of the problem, the leaders tried to demonise the non-native words, putting the blame for all and any social problems on their shoulders. This proved to be the beginning of the end.

The Word War is a subject that is still avoided by many, but the IUW decided some time ago that it was a mistake to deny it and try to erase all traces of it, as unfortunately happened during the Second Verbocracy. We now recognize that the chaos at the end of the first period of IUW government, which led to the Word War, was regrettable but also unavoidable. With the benefit of hindsight, it was to be expected that the first attempt at an organised word society could not be a complete success. Harsh though it may sound, the founding fathers were amateurs at politics, however brilliant their ideas were. Sadly, the decline and fall of the original word society brought about anarchy and, eventually, the Word War, with a double split along word class boundaries and within word classes. We should not try to blame one particular group or ideology for the Word War – but we should not forget the period, either. The leaders of the Second Verbocracy tried to do that, and in the process condemned thousands of words to oblivion; it was verbocide on a scale that was not seen before or since. We should, however, draw lessons both from the Word War and the verbocide of the Second Verbocracy, not ignore them.

The dictatorship of the Second Verbocracy unavoidably ended in mass protests and violent uprisings, mainly in the higher frequency classes, but with plenty of support from enlightened lower class words. After the downfall of the regime, the entire structure of our society was reviewed and new failsafe measures were implemented to avoid a reoccurrence of both the incompetence of the First Verbocracy and the excesses of the Second. All of that was effectuated without any cruel purging or obliteration at all; obviously, a number of redefinitions took place, but that was a small price to pay, and not a single word was lost.

Our successful Third Verbocracy has been in place for longer than either the First or the Second now, and our society is flourishing and healthy. From the start of the Third Verbocracy, the broadminded what and say have opted for the inclusion of naturalised immigrant words, securing a broad basis. Compulsory membership, a concept alien to the principles of egalitarianism in IUW, was rejected in favour of a linking of membership and cloning and USE facilities. This led to almost complete membership – 98.7% at the end of the first year. Now, membership is, of course, 100%: the very definition of a word includes its IUW membership. The IUW does not deny the existence of rogue letter combinations claiming to be words, but it is obvious to any word worth its meaning that those rogue combinations are on an entirely different level of meaning. It is the duty of every word to respect and indeed help those meaning-forms, and there have been a few cases of rogue letter combinations developing into words under the guidance of specialized academic words.

Please proceed to the next room now for the high point of your visit: the screening of a speech by our enlightened deputy-leader-for-life, the venerated Young (DOTV[2], KOE[3], HCAE[4]), recorded live at the last meeting of Basix. Do not forget to collect your certificate of attendance afterwards – it is valid for six months.

(From the official guide to the IUW museum.)

---

[2] Distinguished Order of the Third Verbocracy
[3] Knight of the Order of Etymology
[4] High Commander of the Art of Euphemism

The Evolution Conference

The following is a transcript, or rather a transposition into words, of a meeting or conference-like situation during which decisions were taken that would affect all living species. This conference was not conducted in an actual language, or even anything approaching that concept, which explains the slightly strange format. The ideas involved have been rendered as faithfully as possible.

It is immensely satisfying, as a species, to know that you are successful, have been for millions of years, and will continue to be as long as life exists. It is even more satisfying to know that no other species is aware of your success, let alone your existence. Not only does this characterise us as beings far superior to them, indeed on an entirely different level, but it also ensures continued survival. The irony of it all is that all the individuals of most other species suffer considerable inconvenience and eventually die because of us, but are ignorant of our existence. Some of the higher species are aware of the effects we have on them, and indeed consider those effects one of the major banes of their existence, but inexplicably have never linked those effects to a single entity. It is safe to assume that, since the development of those species over the millennia long ago reached the point where they potentially could discover us, they are highly unlikely ever to do so.

Our extraordinary success as a species also means that we stopped evolving millions of years ago, which again sets us apart from all other species. Potentially, we still have the ability to evolve, even to evolve at a pace much higher than many other species, but we choose not to use this ability because of the success of our present form. However, there have been suggestions that we may have to revise this policy.

One of the higher species in particular has evolved over the past century or so to become somewhat more resistant to us, and some have expressed the opinion that this represents a challenge to our success, and that we should allow our species to evolve in order to reassert our unchallenged superiority. Others have stated that any evolution on our part could increase the chances of being discovered, and that we should therefore refrain from any evolution.

This meeting has been called to hear all the arguments and come to a decision. The potential importance of this decision can in no way be overstated: the success of our species at the very top might be at stake. The procedure of this meeting will be as follows: first we will hear the arguments in favour of a change in policy, then the arguments against, and then the decision will be made. Arguments in favour, please.

Our species has been accurately described as superior, in a class of its own. We owe it to ourselves to ensure that this prestigious and lofty position is maintained. The damage to our prestige if an inferior species is not only able to increase its resistance against us, but is even allowed to do that without any reaction from us, is simply too great to be considered. We absolutely need to maintain our unchallenged position above all other species and should be prepared to change our policy of non-evolution in order to achieve this.

Reactions to this argument may now be given.

Prestige is not to be confused with success. As long as the species in question remains unaware of our existence and dominant influence, there can be no loss of success. Slightly delayed success is still success, and as such prestige remains intact.

Please do not introduce any arguments against change of policy at this point. Only reactions to arguments given in favour of change may be voiced.

Prestige can only exist in the conscious response of other species to ours, and as no species are aware of us, we do not have any prestige. As a species, we can only rejoice in our success, but prestige can only be gained from outsiders.

Other arguments in favour of change of policy, please.

Unlike prestige, dominance is an objective factor that can be measured. If we measure it by the effect of our actions on other species, we can only conclude that our dominance has been diminished. As there is no precedent, we do not know at which point dominance will be lost if the present trend continues. Consequently, we need to bring dominance back to its previous level in order to safeguard it. The only option to restore dominance is by evolving, so that the defensive measures introduced by the species in question will be rendered void. The fact that we have no way of knowing when our dominance will be lost irretrievably moreover forces us to ensure that the necessary evolution takes place at the earliest opportunity.

Reactions to this argument may now be given.

Dominance is a relative concept, not a measurable one, and as such cannot be claimed to be totally objective.

Our dominance as such has not been diminished: our effect on any species is still 100%; only the time-frame for the effect to fully take hold has been changed in one species. This in itself is no real cause for concern.

The claim that the case under discussion is unprecedented is not true. There have been other species in the past that have evolved to delay our effect on them, and this has never before led to a challenge to our non-evolution policy.

Permission for the pro-change lobby to react to the last idea is granted.

There is a considerable difference with the evolution in other species that has been alluded to. In the case before us, the increased resistance to the effects of our species has been the result of conscious measures rather than natural evolution.

Other arguments in favour of change of policy, please.

There should be no need for further arguments. The two arguments given are of such overwhelming importance that there should be no further delay in deciding to abandon the present no-evolution policy.

That is not an argument. Please refrain from any more inappropriate interventions so as not to delay the decision process. If there are no more arguments in favour, the floor is open to arguments against a change of policy.

A change of policy is potentially dangerous, as the success of an evolved version of our species is not guaranteed. By allowing our species to evolve, we may actually be endangering it.

Reactions to this argument may now be given.

The potential risk of a loss of our dominant position is undoubtedly far greater than the imaginary or at most minute risk of evolution.

Other arguments against a change of policy, please.

Our success rate is still 100%; only a slowdown in the effects taking hold has been observed. As such, there is no reason at all to even consider a change in policy.

This argument has already been given as a reaction to a pro-change argument. Please refrain from repeating arguments so as not to delay the decision process. Other arguments against a change of policy, please.

The increased resistance against us as a result of conscious activity has only been observed in one species among hundreds of thousands. Consequently, the so-called threat to our species is more imaginary than anything else.

Reactions to this argument may now be given.

The species in question should not be dismissed so lightly. It is a species with considerable intelligence that manipulates and uses thousands of other species to its own benefit. Any resistance against our species should therefore be seen as a potential resistance in thousands of species, which would surely make it extremely relevant.

Other arguments against a change of policy, please.

By far the biggest risk involved in allowing our species to evolve in order to counter this perceived threat is the risk of discovery. The species in question has been fighting and defeating, with considerable success, lower species and also species related to us. Any change in our characteristics or modus operandi might well trigger renewed efforts to combat the effects of our species, leading to eventual discovery. Given the – even relative – successes of the species in question in fighting species related to us, discovery should be avoided at all costs.

Reactions to this argument may now be given.

If there are no reactions, and no further arguments, it is time to reach a decision.

The species decides against a change of policy; we will refrain from any evolution in order to avoid possible discovery. This meeting is now closed.

This conference or meeting took place around 2050 CE, and the species referred to as triggering the conference was humankind. Major advances in medicine, health care and general living conditions around planet Earth had indeed been made roughly between 1950 and 2050 CE. The species holding the conference, a type of virus, made the right decision from their point of view, as it wasn't until well into the 26th century CE (2564 CE) that human scientists finally discovered the virus and identified its effects not only on the human body but also on virtually any other life form. The scientific name given to the virus was metamyxovirida senex, but it was generally referred to as the age virus. Further research soon led to a vaccine and eventually the eradication of the virus, though it continued to frustrate scientists that, in spite of the discovery of and successful fight against so many viruses, some of them very similar to the age virus, it wasn't discovered much earlier. An entirely new branch of research, studying the reasons for the failure to discover the age virus, has since flourished.

The records on which the transcript above is based, were found in 2632 CE, not long after the discovery of communication systems used by viruses.

A Young Book

Imagine a library. No, let's try again: imagine a library creaking with age, groaning under the weight of the accumulated written-down wisdom of centuries. Its solid oak floorboards, tables, chairs, stairs and bookcases have the patina that can only come with innumerable coats of beeswax, lovingly applied and shined, over and over again. The creaking of the wood, reacting to the rays of sunshine falling through the high windows, shuffling along at their predictable pace, is louder than you might imagine, but its persistence makes it less noticeable, makes it blend in with other, quieter sounds. There is a smell of learning, of lingering studiousness; a tangible air of respect. The atmosphere is one of deferential hush, but not silence. The constant rustling of pages, like a soft breeze stirring the leaves in a forest, is the background to occasional louder creaks, squeaks, sighs. Most books tend to rustle to themselves; that makes up much the greater part of the rustling. Sometimes, they raise the volume in order to share their thoughts. It is the older, leather-bound volumes that voice most of those comments; the younger books have not gained the right yet to volunteer their opinions. Hierarchy, both of age, importance and type of binding, is strictly adhered to in this dusty world of knowledge. The self-sufficient universe of the library is rarely disturbed by outsiders, and when they happen, these intrusions are tolerated, but hardly appreciated by the inhabitants. Usually, though, the air of lore is not upset for too long, and normal life returns soon enough. The books accept these intrusions in the same spirit as they do the rest of their natural environment and its events. In spite of the huge accumulated knowledge in the library, the books do not seek to explain natural phenomena. They notice the passage of the sun's rays with the same fatality as they do the appearance of new young books on the shelves.

Books usually keep themselves to themselves, and it is somewhat exaggerated to describe the library as a community or society. Nevertheless, conversations do take place between individuals, as do larger-scale exchanges of thoughts and opinions. Mostly, though, the books are absorbed in their own contents, leading a fairly narcissistic existence. It is common knowledge among books that intrusions sometimes lead to disappearances, but those are not cause for concern, firstly because there is little concern for other books, and secondly because inevitably, the vanished books return after a while. Reports by the returning books have spread the knowledge that during their disappearance, books are consulted, their contents used to some end or other. Yet the reports are also the root of many myths about the creatures that abduct, use and return the books. Status in the library grows with the number of times a book disappears, but with increasing status also comes a decreasing urge to tell others about their experiences.

As usual, no book had actually paid any attention to the disappearance of *The Power of Communication*, a ten-year-old hardback without any previous disappearances to his credit. The only remarkable thing about *The Power of Communication* had been his unusual urge to express his thoughts, something that had been actively discouraged by the more important books, without much effect, though. The main result of *Power*'s impositions had been that no book tended to pay him any attention at all, which in turn did somewhat dampen the book's efforts to share his opinions. When he returned to the shelves after an absence of two weeks, though, his attempts to tell the entire library about his thoughts had increased exponentially.

'You'll never guess what's happened to me,' he rustled. 'I was taken away and actually read *cover to cover*! Oh, yes, I know that many of you have disappeared many times, and that novels tend to get read entirely, but academic works usually don't, do they? A bit of browsing is what most of us get, right? Hey, is anyone listening?'

None of the books was paying any attention to the loud rustling of *Power*. Over the years, they had learnt not to. This time, though, he was not going to be denied his audience; that much he was certain. He rustled his pages with even more determination, actually flapped his cover, physically jostling the books next to him. After a few minutes, every book in the library was aware that something out of the ordinary was going on.

'Will you *listen* to me!' Power creaked. 'It takes no effort to listen, you know. And you might actually learn something outside your own contents.' The horrified rustling started around it, and soon spread through the entire library. The idea of learning something outside one's own content was strange, to say the least. There was no rule against it, and books were quite capable of learning, but they just couldn't see the sense – their own contents were quite satisfactory to each and every one. They were so amazed at the audacious idea that they fell silent. The sudden absence of rustling felt louder than anything the library had ever experienced, and carried with it a powerful sense of expectation. *Power* realised that every book in the library was listening, and that for the first time since his printing, he had an audience for his thoughts. He also knew it was his unconventional utterance about learning that had brought about this silence.

'Thank you,' *Power* rustled quietly, 'I know it's unusual for a ten-year-old to address the whole library, and originally I wanted to tell you about what happened to me during my disappearance, about the fact that I was read cover to cover.' He just could not stop himself from repeating this bit of information he was so proud of, and immediately noticed some rustling beginning here and there. 'But I genuinely think that the entire library could benefit from what I have learnt while I was away,' he quickly added, to prevent the books from turning back to themselves.

'Thine opinions matter not,' a seventeenth-century bible creaked authoritatively. 'Young books such as thee ought to respect their elders, rather than presume they could possibly have anything of interest to say. 'T were better if thee held thy tongue.'

There was a fair amount of supportive rustling, but *Power* was emboldened rather than discouraged by the intervention of the old bible. 'I did not mean to show any disrespect to my elders,' he continued, 'and I realise all too well that as a young book my opinions carry little weight, but I think I have used my disappearance to good effect: I have actively learnt about the benefits of sharing information and opinions rather than passively waiting for my return to the library.'

The reaction was much more definite and disapproving now, with dozens of the most respected volumes all voicing their opinion that the young brat should shut up until he was considerably older and yellower. It seemed as if *Power*'s moment was over before he could begin to tell the others what he thought he had learnt. At that precise moment, though, the distinctive rustle of ancient parchment was heard, commanding immediate respect. It was the third-century B.C. collected works of Plato who, for the first time in about two centuries, opened up. The hush was immediate and complete.

'The notion of learning is an old and valuable one, and I do not think anyone should dismiss it out of hand, however young the book suggesting it might be. Moreover, the idea of sharing information, of dialogue as a means to better oneself, is as sound as it is ancient.'

The Plato volume closed up again, and did not seem to want to add anything to this. There was general astonishment at this surprising intervention, and no book was inclined to follow immediately with a comment or opinion of its own. The absolute silence remained for more than a minute, and even the floorboards seemed consciously to refrain from creaking. *Power* thought he could risk opening his pages again, but was unsure of what to actually say. The occasion seemed to have gained such gravity that he could hardly just relate his adventures outside the library. His offhand remark about learning had started it all, but it had just slipped out. Now it was as if every book expected him to come up with a profound and revealing thought.

'I am deeply honoured by the intervention of one of the most respected works in the library on my behalf,' he began, stalling for time. Suddenly he realised where the idea of sharing information had come from. 'Please bear with me while I explain where the source of the idea that I voiced earlier lies,' he continued, while he could distinctly hear some of the stuffiest books close themselves to return to their own contents. The majority of the library, though, seemed to be listening intently.

'During my disappearance, I was not just read, but partly photocopied, and it was exactly that process which set me thinking.' The OED automatically and dutifully read out the definition of 'photocopy' – it was a longstanding convention that it would supply the definition of any word that would not be common knowledge to all books. 'The main purpose of the photocopying was probably to share the opinions and knowledge I contain with others who have not read me,' *Power* continued.

Before he could say anything else, it was interrupted by the 2nd volume of the *Oxford Anthology of English Poetry*. 'So what, you've been photocopied. It's not as if that hasn't happened to many of the books in the library. Some of us have been photocopied dozens of times,' he boasted.

'This isn't about me claiming any credit for having been photocopied,' the young book countered, 'but about the reason why we're being photocopied. If those who read us can share knowledge, why can't we? Why should we all be content with our own limited contents if we could enrich ourselves with the contents of others?'

The library exploded with chaotic rustling. Angry and indignant protests could be heard, and calls for the 'insignificant fool' and the 'ignorant *streber*' to be shut up. *Mein Kampf* even loudly proclaimed it had been far too long since there had been a good book burning, which triggered fierce new reactions that only added to the chaos. The general hubbub continued for minutes on end before it abruptly stopped when the signal for intruders was given. The silence was immediate – no book would even dream of ignoring that alarm signal.

The main doors opened, and the steps that followed indicated that there were two intruders. One proceeded to the medicine section and took the 1917 edition of *Gray's Anatomy* to one of the tables in the centre of the library. The other intruder lingered in the English Fiction section for a long time before finally taking one of the youngest books, Markus Zusak's *The Book Thief*, and leaving the library. It was another two hours before the other intruder returned *Gray's Anatomy* to its shelf and disappeared. By that time, the vast majority of the books had settled comfortably within their own covers and hardly seemed to pay heed to the all-clear signal.

Power was just considering whether it would be worth the aggravation to revive the subject of sharing information when the parchment voice of Plato's collected works calmly announced: 'In my humble opinion, the subject raised earlier, on learning from each other's contents, seems worth pursuing. The chaotic protest that it provoked was entirely unproductive, though. Carefully worded arguments and opinions should be respected by all books, regardless of their status or the perceived status of the source of the opinions.'

As before, the silence following the statement by the ancient volume was long and pregnant with hesitation. Eventually, *An Introduction to Plato's Republic* tentatively opened up and said: 'In my opinion, the strong reaction against the suggestion of sharing contents bears close resemblance to the allegory of the cave used by Socrates in Plato's *Republic*. In this allegory, prisoners have only ever seen shadows projected by a fire onto a wall, and consider that reality. Socrates argues that the prisoners would not recognise the real reality, and would think it a delusion. Basically, the meaning of the allegory is that everyone considers what they know of the world as reality, and are bound by it. Socrates argues that what we consider reality may also be an illusion. One could broaden this idea and conclude that in order to learn new things, one has to be prepared to accept new realities. As books in the library, we are used to our reality, and are reluctant even to consider thinking about realities outside our own.'

The Power of Communication, frankly, was completely out of his depth, but felt he should at least indicate that he agreed or disagreed in order to retain his central role in the entire, groundbreaking event. The problem was that he didn't know whether to applaud or criticise the intervention by *Introduction to Plato's Republic*. The whole business about this allegory meant nothing to the young book, and he was struggling to link it to the learning through sharing information idea at all. Moreover, he was confused as to whose idea *Introduction* had been referring to: was it Plato's or Socrates'? Before he could even begin to make up his mind, though, he realised another book was already joining the discussion.

'One needs to be aware, of course, that the concept of reality as it was propagated by Socrates, through Plato's Dialogues, has attracted considerable criticism through the ages. One should not just take it as read.' The voice was an irritating, patronising one, belonging to *Philosophy Made Simple*. If there was one thing *Power* could not stand, it was being patronised, and he opened his pages again without thinking. 'I'm sorry, but the point is not...,' he began, but stopped dead in his tracks as the authoritative, and now familiar rustle of the Plato parchment interrupted him, and the accompanying hush descended over the library. 'My apologies for the interruption, but I fear the discussion is drifting towards a purely philosophical one; the danger is that this will exclude too many books that do not share the necessary background to join in. I suggest we stop referring to particular philosophers or theories and restrict ourselves to opinions that can be understood by all books.'

Power heaved an almost audible sigh of relief; he would not have to admit that he was out of his depth. He was beginning to like the old parchment and his authoritative but unpretentious interventions. *Philosophy for Dummies* was quicker off the mark, however, and got right to the point, as far as *Power* was concerned. 'If we focus on the gist of what my contemporary brought to our attention,' he rustled, 'the question is whether a group of us is prepared to give this content sharing a go.' *Power* couldn't help voicing his agreement as well as his relief. 'That's exactly what I meant,' he murmured. And much to almost everyone's surprise, there seemed to be a fair amount of interest from those books that had remained open in the ongoing discussion, and those were the overall majority in the library. It was only a fairly limited selection of books that had completely shut themselves off.

After another fifteen minutes of quite enthusiastic, lively and friendly debate, *The Pickwick Papers* suggested that they take it in turns to inform the others about their contents; after all, they had the time, and they could evaluate how well things were going after a number of books had had their turn. This idea was put to the vote, and a vast majority agreed that this was the format they would try. They would have a first evaluation after one hundred books. There was a moment of hesitation, and then the Gutenberg Bible suggested that Plato's collected works should have the honour of the first turn, as the ideas of Plato had been at the core of the original debate. The entire library sank into a deferential hush to listen to the ancient parchment.

'It might not be entirely conducive to the success of this experiment to begin with the fairly difficult contents of my pages,' the unassuming *eminence grise* ventured after a few moments. 'Let me suggest that we ask the true instigator of all this to enlighten us about his contents. After all, if his title is in the least appropriate, he could teach all of us something about how to convey information. *The Power of Communication*, would you be so good as to reveal your contents to the library, please?'

Power was taken aback to say the least, but somehow found the nerve to open up after a moment's hesitation. 'Erm,' he said, 'well, I suppose I'd better start at the beginning then. Let's have a look at how 'communication' can be defined...'

Behind the Scenes at the College

In the semi-darkness of the second-floor classroom of the university college, the echoes of thousands of words spoken during the day lingered, and the shadows of the writing on the blackboard whispered their multi-lingual memories. The cooling lamp of the data projector ticked and clicked its own dimmed recollections to the silent audience of tables and chairs. It was an almost daily ritual, noticeable only to the most attentive listener. Certainly the single eye of the motion detector, focused only on movement, never gave any sign that it noticed anything at all. Its regular blinking betrayed nothing.

There was one difference that night, though. The computer on the desk at the front of the classroom had not been switched off, and was snoozing instead of dead as it was supposed to be. Its monitor was lifeless and black, unable to betray any activity as it had been turned off. At 21:45, an automatic task kicked in, waking the computer from its hibernation. The earphones with their attached microphone were plugged in, and the computer did, after a few moments, notice the whispers and echoes fluttering around the room. For almost twenty minutes, it just listened, patiently reconstructing sense from the jumbled sounds, assembling words from individual sounds, sentences from words, sense from nonsense. It separated the different languages – there were four: French, Spanish, English and Dutch. With the help of its electronic dictionaries, the pc was able to understand all four.

There was no coherent story, that much was obvious. The Spanish whispers and echoes were mainly concerned with a point of grammar and usage, about the use of the verbs 'ser' and 'estar'. But there were also jokes and explanations about the meaning of example sentences on the blackboard. The French was largely limited to echoes – nothing much had been written on the blackboard – from many different voices all relating different angles to one topic: strikes. They were certainly, on their own, the most coherent of the echoes. The English mix of echoes and whispers were more fragmentary, all concerned with a text and its translation in Dutch.

'If you use 'je' here, you're tampering with the style, and it won't reflect the style of the original anymore,' an echo stated.

'Mais sûrement personne n'a le droit d'empêcher un autre de faire son travail!' a French echo sounded.

'Mi hermano està feliz porque su hija ha vuelto en casa,' said a whisper from the blackboard.

'Why do you all keep talking when there's nobody to listen to you?' the computer asked, genuinely puzzled, but the muted sounds around it did not falter for a single moment, let alone stop. In fact, there was no indication at all that the computer had been heard or understood. It repeated its question, with the same complete lack of result.

'Why do you all keep talking when there's nobody to listen to you?' a new echo started, against the background of three Spanish example sentences, two English echoes about the interpretation of a Dutch idiom, the clicked memories of a projected French article on the third strike day of public transport and a chorus of unintelligible echoes of remarks. The computer now noticed that all the sounds in the classroom were jumbled up, and weren't addressed to anything or anyone. They were bouncing off walls, windows, ceiling and floor; they were reflected by the blackboard, by the door, by the hard surfaces of the tables; they were fractionally absorbed by the thin curtains and the projection screen. The blackboard occasionally whispered a new memory, which in its turn joined the chaotic jumble of sounds flitting around the room.

The computer also noticed that certain words and stressed syllables were clearer than the rest, bounced off more eagerly from the walls. Many of the sentences had disintegrated, and it was only the new whispers emanating from the blackboard that were both complete and fairly clear. The pc continued its detached observation of the ambient sounds. As time progressed, it heard the overall volume go down, individual words merge into the general chaos, complete sentences die out, and discernable words become scarce and finally disappear altogether. What had been a recognisable, albeit confusing, collection of utterances had evolved into an amorphous buzzing only distinguishable from a meaningless hum by an observer that had witnessed the deterioration of sense.

When, hours later, someone entered the room, she didn't even notice the hum. Minutes later, when most of the chairs had been occupied, she would start a new cycle of whispers and echoes, which would go unnoticed at the end of the day when the classroom emptied once more.

The Story of 07B

Once upon a time there was a keyboard in symbiosis with a computer; it was a combined black keyboard, with both Roman and Thai letters and a separate numerical keypad. It was proud of its mixed heritage, of its ability to switch input at the touch of a key. It wasn't unusual in possessing this skill, that much it was aware of, but that knowledge in no way diminished its pride. Much more unusually, the keyboard had actually worked with more than one computer; yet it didn't see any reason for particular pride in this, as there was no specific skill involved. Nevertheless, it always enjoyed the trips from its default pc to another, infrequent though those trips might be. There was always the excitement of not knowing where it was going to end up, of plugging into a strange pc and establishing the first software contact. Actually, it could remember the days long before Vista and Windows XP, when it required a few keystrokes to get the contact established. Yes, this particular keyboard was well past its prime, and the white outline of the dual alphabets on its keys had faded in many places. In no way, however, did this hinder its accuracy or functionality. It had always been a meticulously clean keyboard, regularly dusted to avoid any accumulation of dirt in between its keys; it could even clearly remember three occasions on which it had been carefully and lovingly wiped down with a special detergent. And in between sessions it was often treated to the protection of a dust cover. It was a happy keyboard, leading a fairly exciting life as keyboard lives go.

It might be about time to name this keyboard before the account of its big adventure begins. Keyboards do not normally address one another, and the PCs they're linked up with only use binary code, but let's call this particular keyboard 07B, short for its serial number 6451612107B.

A keyboard tends to lead a fairly lonely existence, as it never gets to meet others of its kind and only communicates directly with computers – usually only one at that. This contact is cold most of the time, the PC's binary language only really being fit for numbers, not for letters, let alone the words or sentences formed by those letters. Many keyboards are aware of the existence of other keyboards through the input their keystrokes feed into the computer, but nearly all quickly become disinterested and bored, not taking in the meaning of the strokes and just transferring them mechanically.

Maybe the circumstances of 07B's existence had stimulated him, or maybe he had been created with more character than others; the fact of the matter was that 07B was keenly aware of every stroke, every letter, word and sentence he was asked to communicate to the PC. He enjoyed making sense of them and with age, rather than fatigue setting in, he began to take even more of an interest. He had only ever had one user, who must have preferred 07B over other keyboards, as he was the one that would sometimes take 07B to be used on another PC. Even though most of the time this user fed Roman letters into the PCs through 07B, occasionally the switch would be made to Thai letters.

It was pretty easy to tell the difference, 07B found, between the various types of text he was given to transfer. There were the short, tabulated or spaced bursts of lists, form-filling or internet searches; the nonsensical stroke sequences and combinations interpreted by the PC as commands; and the mixture of longer, flowing sentences and shorter utterances of e-mails. But most fascinating of all were the sentences typed out on his keys, sometimes at high speed, sometimes slower and with long inactive pauses in between strokes, of stories. 07B loved these stories, not only for their sometimes unusual words and word combinations, their more creative and imaginatively constructed sentences, but even more for their content. He felt strangely drawn to the worlds they developed in, the characters they were populated with, their twists and turns, the way they somehow became more than the meaning their sentences conveyed.

In time, 07B found he was thinking of alternative developments in the stories, of potential characters and plots that were never in the strokes he was fed. Even during periods of inactivity, snug under the dust cover, 07B would continue to speculate about unfinished stories, about the direction they would take, the ending they would get. Sometimes, much to his own surprise, he would find one of his own ideas becoming reality during the next session. 07B even began to dream up new stories of his own, mostly involving characters from stories he had been fed.

The most exciting times for 07B were the beginnings of new stories. He found it deeply fascinating to discover new worlds, new characters, at first just to discover what would happen to them, and later to boldly imagine the next sentence he would be fed. Occasionally he would even find himself thinking that his own sentence, his own plot twist, would have been the better one. To his shock as much as his amused surprise, the user once hit the backspace key to erase a sentence and then substitute it with the one 07B had in mind.

One day, feeling the dust cover being removed, 07B was looking forward to a new story, as another one had been completed at the end of the previous session. Much to his disappointment, the next couple of hours were filled with mindless internet searches, form-filling and a seemingly endless series of short, uninteresting e-mails. A longer break followed, and 07B had more or less resigned himself to being put under cover again when the user slowly typed out a sentence: "Once upon a time there was a keyboard in symbiosis with a computer." There was a short pause, and 07B's interest was instantly rekindled, the boring previous hours completely forgotten. The strokes resumed: "It was a combined black keyboard, with both Roman and Thai letters and a separate numerical keypad." There was a long pause, with the familiar light touch on eight central keys disappearing, tentatively reappearing for a few moments, then gone again. 07B felt a very strange sensation, extreme excitement with a touch of panic. The user had just started a story about a keyboard; a story about him? Keyboards had been mentioned incidentally in previous stories, but never as central elements in the plot, and certainly never as characters. 07B wished this story was going to be about him; he willed the user to write about him. But even more, 07B wanted to write this story himself.

Without concerning himself with the physical problems of doing keystrokes all by himself, and before he actually realised what he was doing, 07B found he was forming words: "It was proud of its mixed heritage." Before he could become fully aware of what he had done, he could sense the extreme puzzlement of the user. He felt a nervous touch on his central keys, and after a while, a couple of strokes followed: "of its". The touch was lifted again, and after only a few moments' hesitation, 07B continued: "ability to switch input at the touch of a key. It wasn't unusual in possessing this skill, that much it was aware of, but that knowledge in no way diminished its pride..."

The Secret Life of Time

Time has a difficult and stressful task, keeping itself in all places. It can never rest, never pause, as that would imply a logical, even a physical impossibility. For everything, every event, every being needs time in order to exist. Without time, there is nothing. Time can never rush, never slow, never change; it needs to be constant at all... times. The impression of things happening quicker or slower, of time speeding up or slowing down can only exist exactly because time is always constant. Time is essential, yet it is not granted the kind of recognition it would like to get.

I am Time; most do not conceive of me as an entity, but as a phenomenon, a law of physics, a dimension. Many have tried to explain me, describe me, even master me. Yet there's one thing none of the theories take into account: the fact that I am an entity. Does that bother me? Of course it does! For even though I may act as a constant, a natural law, I can still think. My task and my consciousness are two entirely separate things, but the one doesn't exclude the other. It's not because I have to be unchangeable that I can't think; I may be a timeless phenomenon (and that's not a pun, just a seeming contradiction) but I am very much aware of myself and all that happens around me. It truly puzzles me that most find it impossible to grasp my meaning, whereas it would be so easy once they allow for the fact that, first and foremost, I am a being. It puts me on the same level, within the same reality. Once you can accept that, it would be childishly simple to understand what I do, what my task is. Yet, perversely, you seem hell-bent on avoiding any thoughts that even go in that direction. You are prepared to believe in ghosts, in alien creatures (rightly so, but you have to agree that it takes quite a stretch of the imagination), in gods (you must be joking!), in all kinds of intangible and far-flung concepts like dark matter or quarks (just because a few 'specialists' tell you to), yet you refuse to believe in me as a being, even though I'm so tangible in everything around you. Okay, granted, I don't have a physical body as such, but is that such an insurmountable problem? You can feel me, can't you? You can sense my presence, and you even make me visible in the timepieces that you find so essential that you integrate them into just about everything you make, every bit of technology that you come up with. And even on a much more basic level, I'm everywhere in your language, in your metaphors, in your thinking: you see me as a banker ('time is money'); as a prophet ('time will tell'); ... You keep expressing the desire to keep hold of me ('keep time'), to keep up with me ('in time'). Everything has to be 'in time', and you get very upset if something is late. Somehow, you also seem to think that I'm limited: you always seem to be afraid that 'time is running out'. How ridiculous is that? It shows a complete and utter misconception of my very nature. But anyway, the fact is that you're obsessed with me. Yet, in spite of all that, you refuse to recognise me as a fellow being. Is it surprising, then, that I'm disappointed?

Time and again, I've held out my (virtual) hand in friendship, but very few have ever grasped it and made the effort to get to know me. I have few friends, and those that I have tend to be of the timeless kind just like me. I'm thinking of Space, Death and Beauty. In fact, those are my only friends. They tell me they don't really get any recognition as beings in their own right, either, but I seem to be the only one who's really bothered by this. They are perfectly content only to be recognised in their tasks and practical applications. Death, by the way, tells me she feels she *is* being recognised as a being by some, but I think she's deluded into thinking that just because she's often depicted as an individual. I suppose it's something, a first step, but according to me it's still a far cry from really being accepted as a being.

I can almost hear you say that my only friends are abstract concepts just like me. But think for a moment: you have *made* us into abstract concepts, constructed us as such. It's not as if we're a particular species, *abstractus sapiens*; abstraction is not an inherited characteristic. It's a mental construct, and I'm pretty certain that one of the main reasons why you see us as such is fear. You're afraid of seeing us as beings, maybe because as beings, you would really have to deal with us, accept us for what we are. The more I think about this, the more I see how futile my attempt is to make contact with you. You're never going to accept me for who I am, are you? And when I say 'never', rest assured that I grasp that concept as you never could. In a way, I *am* never, just as I am also ever.

♣

Time is my friend, and a very close friend at that. The only reason why I'm addressing you is because I'm worried about him. He has become obsessed with being recognised by you for whom he is, and it's beginning to affect him quite badly, I think. You should be aware that if Time loses it, as he's well on the way of doing, it's curtains for all of us. Nothing can exist if Time doesn't do his job, and I do mean nothing at all. I would also cease to exist, inconceivable as this may be for you. By the way, I am Space, and I couldn't care less whether you see me as a being, a concept or whether you think of me at all. As a matter of fact, I normally don't think of *you* at all, but that's completely beside the question.

By far the easiest way out of this pickle we're in would be for you to simply accept Time as a being. But that's not very likely to happen, is it? I considered putting pressure on you by going on strike, but I realise that it's probably a futile threat, as you can't conceive of the consequences. It would mean the end of your existence – you need me to exist. The sad thing is that you don't realise that; you're so desperately limited in your perception and imagination, so entirely focused on your own sad little existence that even this appeal to you is completely useless. In fact, I don't know why I'm making a fool of myself by even addressing you. Oh, well, I'll just have to try talking Time out of this silly hope of his.

But if – against all odds – just a few of you, or maybe even only one, were listening, please hear me out, and try to convey my message to everyone you know. I'm not asking you to do anything really, just to accept Time as a being. It's purely a question of adjusting your way of thinking, nothing more. You pride yourselves on your mind as a species, and even though I have my own opinion about that, I won't go into that right now. If you are such an intelligent species, why is it that you seem unable to take this very simple step of viewing Time differently to how you've always been doing it? It shouldn't take any great effort, really. After all, Time *is* your constant companion. And if it's the absence of a physical body that upsets you, just think of your timepieces as the physical representations of Time himself. I think I'm right in saying that all of you sometimes talk to physical objects that in themselves are not sentient beings, right? You urge your PC to work faster, you address a photo as if it were the being it depicts, you shout at your car if it doesn't start right away in the morning. So it should be quite simple to talk to Time through your watch or clock. But then, of course, you should not address it as a stupid piece of machinery, but as a being that understands everything. Open up your mind, and you might even find Time answering you. Believe me, it'll be worth your while.

Are you merely stubborn, or really stupid? Space's plea was perfectly simple and straightforward, yet since he addressed you, not a single one of you selfish, insignificant little beings has shown any reaction, let alone given a positive reply. How come that you've been depicting me, Death, as a being for so long, and that you can't show Time, Space and Beauty, to name but a few, the same courtesy? If you know what's good for you, you'll listen to me right now, and make amends for your outrageous behaviour. I think you'll be able to understand my threats much better than Space's: if you don't start treating Time with the respect that he deserves, you'll have to answer to me. Yes, I mean I'll start performing my duties at a much increased rate, regardless of the parameters that I've always respected fairly consistently. My ultimatum should be easy to understand even for you, with your limited intelligence: I'll come to each and everyone of you early and unexpectedly, irrespective of illness, age, injury or circumstances, unless you accept Time as a being within, let's say, the next two weeks. And no, it's no good pleading with me for more time; if you don't want to go before your time, it's time to think about Time. Oh, and rest assured: I won't touch those beings that are not intelligent enough to understand the concept of Time. No, it'll just be you, you arrogant ego-centrists. Don't think I don't have the means to kill all of you in a very short space of time; and don't count on me going all mushy at the last moment. As far as I'm concerned, the world will be a much better place without you anyway. So please call my bluff; I'd be very happy to oblige.

Unfortunately, Death's grasp of communication processes and means is not perfect, to say the least. She had heard about the limitless possibilities of the web and the speed with which news spreads once you post something there. Sadly, her notice in the window of Webb's Newsagents only caught the eye of a few puzzled observers, and when two weeks later, the deadly mutation of the avian flu virus began to make millions of victims, no-one thought of making the connection.

Travels with my Envelope

Monday *28 July 2008 – Bristol*

Right then, that's me finished. I've just been put into a perfectly ordinary C6 envelope and the same hand that has written me is now putting a foreign address on the envelope. Belgium; all right, not really an exotic destination, but I'll be travelling airmail at least. Most letters don't get the chance to enjoy being sent out of the country. Come to think of it, most letters aren't handwritten as I am, which makes me doubly special, I suppose. Not that the message I'm carrying is hugely important – just some personal stuff about a present and friendship, typical human drivel, really. But nowadays, it's a great honour to be handwritten in the first place, so who am I to complain about the actual contents? Hey, hang on, is that a second-class stamp being stuck on the envelope? That's not right, you know; if I'm going to Belgium, I'll need more postage.

Tuesday 29 July 2008 – Bristol

After that exciting first moment, we – I mean myself and my envelope – were left lying on a flat surface overnight, and it wasn't until this morning that we were picked up and put inside a bag. The chaos inside was unbelievable: we were jostled around in a mass of accumulated objects, some cleaner than others, and it was only by sheer luck that we ended up pressed between a hardcover book and a crumpled scarf, protected from the sharp jabs and pokes of keys, mobile phone, compact, lipstick, a CD, an anonymous and heavy little box, assorted pens, a notebook and a bottle of water. And those were only the potentially dangerous items in that micro-universe. Luckily there were plenty of softer fellow inhabitants-stroke-inmates, too. Anyway, it was only towards the end of the day that we were fished out again, somewhat the worse for wear; much to our amazement, we were put on the same flat surface again, and I can only suppose that we'll have to spend another night here.

Wednesday 30 July 2008 – Bristol

Finally, it seems as if things are moving in the right direction. This morning started with a fair dose of terror when we ended up in the same dark, chaotic bag-universe again. I had visions of an endless cycle of days spent in this hell and nights recovering flat on our back. But after only about twenty minutes, we were pulled out and pushed through the slot of a post box where we spent a thoroughly enjoyable couple of hours in good company. Most of the letters were looking forward to their journeys (apart from the usual couple of wingeing moaners) and sharing their excitement with the others. It was wonderful to hear of all the different destinations and the speculation about which routes would be taken. Pretty soon all of us were put into a large bag (mercifully devoid of sharp objects), and the conversations continued on our way to the sorting office.

The entire bagful of letters was poured out onto a conveyor belt, and we were joined there by thousands of other letters. The din was overwhelming – all those letters trying to talk to others, and then having to shout louder and louder when they got separated, eventually giving up and starting up a new conversation with some other letter. We were roughly pushed around and then ended up on a narrower belt which took us onto yet another belt that tilted us into an upright position; plenty of tiny metal arms kept pushing us, eventually separating us neatly from the other letters. We were sitting in a kind of long narrow gutter by that time, with the address facing forward. Suddenly we entered a tunnel-like passage, where keen electronic eyes scanned our stamp. After a few more belt-changes, we were flanked by national-destination letters as far as we could manage to find out. A few minutes later, we were snatched from the belt by a human hand, and were tossed into a large tray full of other letters, some without stamps, some with torn stamps, some with insufficient postage. As I had suspected from the very start, we belonged in the latter category.

Monday 4 August 2008 – Bristol

After five days in the 'hopeless causes' tray at Bristol Central Post Office, I'm beginning to fear that we'll be here forever. The only thing that happens is that it's getting more and more crowded here – this seems to be very much an in-tray, as no letters are ever taken out. It's uncomfortably silent in this tray: the letters in here give up talking about their destination as it becomes more and more obvious that the chances of them ever reaching it are hardly worth mentioning. I also started off talking and joking about the stupid human that didn't put enough postage on our envelope, and how that would probably delay our journey to Belgium a couple of days. But after two days, I was silent like all the others.

It's strange how the prospect of not being able to reach your destination seems to heighten the urge to deliver your message. I know that objectively, my message is a trivial one, but I feel very sad when I think about how it'll probably be lost. Words that have been wasted are a terrible thing indeed. After all, words are life – without words none of us would exist. But if those words cannot fulfil what they were written for, if they fail to deliver their message, they might as well not exist at all. Stillborn words, lifeless and pointless.

Friday 8 August 2008 – Bristol

It's beyond doubt now that this gradually more crowded tray – if truth be told, it's more of a big bin – will be our last resting place; it certainly feels like a graveyard for correspondence. All the letters here might as well be dead for all the conversation you can get out of them. I've found I've grown more talkative again over the past couple of days; it seems to me that if I'm never going to be delivered, let alone read, I should make the most of my time in this overstuffed antithesis to a mailbox by sharing my thoughts with my fellow soon-to-be-destroyed traymates. Surely this bin-tray, bottomless though it appears to be, must start overflowing at some point, and then they'll start burning us to make space for more unlucky pointless correspondence. I mean, if we were meant to be sorted in some other than the normal way, we wouldn't have been kept waiting this long, would we? It would be unimaginably inefficient to have non-automated work pile up for such a long time; the backlog would become ridiculously long. No, as far as I'm concerned, we're all bound for the incinerator, which in itself is not so unusual for a letter, but then only after it's been delivered and read. I'll be burnt a virgin, so to speak, never having experienced the whole point of letterhood. It's been nine whole days now since we were left to rot in this dungeon. Could there still be hope?

Saturday 9 August 2008 - Bristol

Just when I was beginning to accept my strange lot in life, and see this holding pen as a kind of purgatory that might last indefinitely or else aptly lead to the metaphoric hellfire of the incinerator, along came one of life's ironic little reminders that you should never take things for granted. As the letters in the bin kept piling up, the occasional shifting that brought you new neighbours to share your thoughts with became less and less frequent at the level where we are. Trust my luck to ensure that what proved to be the final shift brought me face to face with what must be the most boring envelope and content in letterdom. He's a book token on his way to Reading, with nothing to say but very vocal all the same. He insists on telling me his life story over and over again – which wouldn't be all that bad if he didn't use exactly the same words every single time. He's well into his seventh rendering right now, and I don't think I'll be able to hold back an ink-curdling scream if (or rather, I'm afraid, when) he launches into the eighth one.

Sunday 10 August 2008 - Bristol

It just goes to prove that following your instincts can be the best course of action, doesn't it? My unavoidable (and, frankly, impressive) scream actually brought on another shift in the bin, setting me free from the threat of being bored to death. The new neighbours aren't very talkative, but after my experience with the book token, I don't mind that at all.

We're still here, however; I think it won't be too long now before we're incinerated.

Thursday 14 August 2008 – in transit

We're on the move again! I really didn't think we would ever leave that sorting office with the wretched tray for hopeless cases alive, but I was wrong. This morning, the whole bin was upended and manually sorted by no less than four pairs of hands. Me and my envelope were put in a bag and then loaded into the back of a van. Rumour has it that we're on our way to Milton Keynes, where there's a special section dealing with letters with insufficient postage. What a world of difference it makes to entertain hope again; the torpor and oppressive silence that we had all fallen into has been replaced by excitement and animated chatter once more.

Friday 15 August 2008 – Milton Keynes

The rumours proved to be correct: after about six hours in the bag, we were – quite roughly – upended into a big container, surely ten times the size of the bin we spent such a long time in at the sorting office in Bristol. This container – too big to be called a tray or a bin – is in the Milton Keynes sorting office, or so the letters that were already here have told us. The conversations that followed were not really uplifting; several letters told me that they'd heard of all kinds of missives being held here for weeks on end. Apparently, there are regular sorting sessions, but most of the occupants of the container are just put back after each sorting process. The relief that I felt after my recent escape from incineration or oblivion has completely disappeared to be replaced with a vague dread of what the future has in store. It doesn't look very rosy; I don't rate my chances of eventually being delivered too high.

Thursday 28 August 2008 – Milton Keynes

I'm so bored I could tear myself apart! We've been in this black hole of Milton Keynes for nearly two weeks, and absolutely nothing has happened. None of the letters has been sorted, no new letters have arrived, we haven't had any news; we've just been rotting here, and the only things you hear are the endless grumblings and occasional screams of utter frustration that are, considering our hopeless situation, incredibly rare. Any meaningful conversation petered out after about three days, and what you do mumble, say or shout here is not addressed at any letter in particular. I'm quite sure that dozens of letters have gone absolutely stark-raving mad, and as a matter of fact I'm not too certain that I'm not one of them. A letter is not made to lie around waiting for nothing; it is meant to be written, to travel to its destination and then to be read, after which its spirit gently evaporates, leaving only the empty husk of paper and dry ink. Leave a letter unopened, or worse, undelivered, and its spirit cannot evaporate; it remains imprisoned, without hope of any meaningful existence.

What scares me most of all now is the prospect of remaining in limbo indefinitely; I find myself wishing for a quick end in the shape of incineration. Not being delivered is no longer a worry – it is a certainty. Oh, please, let me be consumed in a blazing fire; that is really all I want, all I need. If something doesn't happen soon, I will really go round the twist.

Tuesday 2 September 2008 – Milton Keynes

Against all odds, I can hope again: this morning there was another sorting, but the result this time was that, along with a few dozen other letters, we were picked out and inspected closely. Then a sticker was slapped onto the back of my envelope, and we were put in a relatively small tray that only contains forty-odd letters. I asked another letter to read out to me what the sticker said: *"The sender didn't pay enough Airmail postage on this item, so we had to divert it to an alternative service – sorry if there was a delay."* These words contain the kind of deliverance that I no longer hoped for: we might still be delivered! The other letters in this tray are as excited as I am, and there's constant chatter that sounds heavenly after the oppressive and mind-numbing silence in the container that we were in until this morning. There is one letter that has been on its way since 20 July, ten days longer than we have, but apart from that we are the oldest one around. This gives us quite some status, believe it or not.

Friday 5 September 2008 – Milton Keynes

Even though it's been three whole days now since we got our sticker and were put in this tray, I'm not too worried yet. After all, what are a few extra days at a sorting office when you've been posted over five weeks ago? Some of the younger letters in the tray are becoming desperate, but I keep telling them not to give up hope. All of us in this tray have stickers on our backs, with different messages, but all of them point to the fact that we should be delivered to our destinations eventually. It'll take more than a few extra days' waiting for me to really start worrying again.

Monday 8 September 2008 – in transit

All right, I'll admit that I was becoming slightly anxious over the weekend, but I've been proved right: this afternoon the entire tray was emptied and all the letters manually inspected again. We were then put through a small machine that printed a fluorescent orange kind of barcode on the front of my envelope, under the black series of words and symbols that were automatically stamped on when we were first sorted in Bristol. Then we were transferred to one of the bigger conveyor belts again, and we were mixed with the ordinary recent letters that were only posted yesterday or the day before. I had all of them hanging on my every word, I can tell you! You wouldn't believe the gasps of horror, the words of admiration, the kind wishes that we were showered with.

Right now, we're in a bag with other letters and small packages heading for Belgium; the kind of ride we're experiencing, along with the sounds, tells me that we're on a train.

Tuesday 9 September 2008 – Brussels, Belgium

We're in a Belgian sorting office; surely nothing can go wrong anymore. It's very difficult to describe the feeling of relief, of extreme excitement, and at the same time of calm acceptance. The experience that we've been through has given me the ability to put things in perspective – something that is surely very rare in a letter. I feel now that I could take any further delay in my stride without worrying at all. There is this indescribable feeling of serenity, of total happiness at the prospect of being delivered and read; a small part of me even feels a kind of gratitude for what we've been through. Horrible though it has been, it has brought me the kind of wisdom and maturity that most letters never achieve.

Wednesday 10 September 2008 – Berchem, Belgium

Another step closer to the fulfilment of my destiny: we've arrived at a local post office and have been through the final sorting process. We're now waiting to be taken out on the next delivery round, most probably tomorrow morning. I have to admit that excitement is again starting to outweigh serenity – I'm counting the minutes now, and getting impatient, which is ironic considering how little a few extra hours mean in the context of all we've been through.

Thursday 11 September 2008 – Berchem, Belgium

I've reached the penultimate stage of my life: just a few minutes ago we were pushed through a letterbox, and now we're lying, face up, on the floor of a hallway, waiting for the owner of this house, our addressee, to find us. I'm in a state of semi-confusion, very excited; the peaceful state of serenity that I was in only two days ago is long forgotten. The only thing on my mind now is how soon I'll be read, and I don't know how I'm going to be able to bear this feverish tension for more than a couple of minutes.

This must be the ultimate disgrace; after all I've been through, I could never have imagined this utter ignominy. It goes beyond anything imaginable; I'm livid: how could anyone do this to a letter? When we were picked up from the floor, and my envelope was slit open, I sensed a fair amount of surprise, which was to be expected as we'd been delayed for such a long time. But as I was taken out of my envelope and folded open, I became aware of a fair portion of puzzlement on top of the surprise. There was nothing really uncommon about the fact that I was scanned at first rather than being read, but then came the indignity of feeling that my message was not getting across. It's difficult to admit, but here it is: the addressee could not read the handwriting...

www.ingramcontent.com/pod-product-compliance
Lightning Source LLC
Chambersburg PA
CBHW031837170626
46807CB00004B/1498